D1562734

Good Girls Love Thugs 2

By

Shvonne Latrice

Text LEOSULLIVAN to 22828 to join our mailing list!

To submit a manuscript for our review, email us at

leosullivanpresents@gmail.com

© 2015

Published by Leo Sullivan Presents

www.leolsullivan.com

All rights reserved.

This is a work of fiction. Names, characters, businesses, places, events and incidents are either the products of the author's imagination or used in a fictitious manner. Any resemblance to actual persons, living or dead, or actual events is purely coincidental. Unauthorized reproduction, in any manner, is prohibited.

Chapter One: Jessica Leon

When Nic told us that Kendrick was hit by a car, we all rushed outside to head to the hospital. Nic hurriedly buckled KJ in his car seat, as the rest of us piled into the car. I offered to drive her, because she was too shaken up to do it herself in my opinion. I sped to Sinai Hospital on Belvedere Avenue as quickly as I could, praying that Kendrick was okay.

Once we arrived, everyone was there. Nic was walking fast as hell, in heels and all, with KJ in tow.

"What's going on?! Where is he?!" she yelled with tears in her eyes, looking back and forth between the brothers.

"The doctor hasn't said anything yet," Kendon responded sadly.

Christy went and sat by Kayden, and he put his arm around her. Morgan did the same with Kendreeis. I walked to Kendon, sat next to him, and held his hand. The doctor finally came out after about an hour and 45 minutes of waiting. Nic shot out her seat.

"Is this Mr. King's family?" he asked, staring at us.

"Yes!" we all said as if were reading from a script we all knew.

"Mr. King is not dead, but he is in a coma," the doctor exhaled, as if to say it didn't look good. Nic broke into tears immediately. The doctor looked at her with sympathy.

"He was getting in his car when a truck flew by very closely, hitting him. Kendrick flew onto the hood of his car, rolled off, and hit the ground. He's been out cold ever since. A bystander who called 911 recounted the events for us," he continued. "We are not sure that he will wake up at this point, but as usual, we are hopeful."

"No God! My baby!" Nic was crying so hard that I thought she was going to pass out.

"Whomever the fuck did this shit is getting bodied! I put that on my fucking life, man! And anybody associated or in my fucking way during the process is going down too!" Kendreeis yelled with tears streaming down his face. Morgan hugged him tight, and you could tell it made him feel good to be in her arms. I was holding Nic as she drenched my shirt with tears. Whomever did this had beyond hell to pay.

Chapter One: Morgan Garrett

Kendrick had been in a coma for weeks now, and I was worried about Nic. She didn't want to do anything but cry all night and go visit Kendrick. My heart broke for her, because I knew she was lost without him. I decided to go visit her and make sure she was okay. I arrived at her house and texted her to let her know I was there.

"Hey," she said dryly as she opened the door.

"Hey, how are you feeling?" I asked, closing the door behind me.

She didn't respond as I followed her into the den. We sat on the couch and watched KJ move around the area in his walker.

"Nic, I'm sorry," was all I said before she burst into tears. I pulled her close and hugged her tight.

"Shhhh, I know," I said as I rubbed her back.

After she got it all out, she sat back up. "Morgan, I'm so sad and I shouldn't be, because I need to be strong for KJ," she said through sniffles.

"Yes you can be Nic, don't hold all that in. It's not good for you," I told her with tears starting to well up. I was one of those people that couldn't watch others cry, or I would cry too.

"I miss him so much," she said quietly, breaking down. I hated to see her like this. I couldn't imagine if Kendreeis was laid up in the hospital in a coma right now, especially with me being pregnant.

"Nic, he is gonna make it through, don't worry."

"That's not what the doctors are saying," she said, chuckling and letting the tears fall.

"Well, what are they saying?"

"They said his heart is getting weaker and weaker, and he is showing no signs of waking up anytime soon," she replied, holding her eyelids tightly together to hold in the tears. "His mother was there too, and we both cried for what seemed like forever. His father is furious," she continued as she grabbed a tissue.

"Yeah so is Dreeis, he is out constantly trying to get revenge for Kendrick. I'm not gon' tell him what the doctors told you, because that may push him over the edge," I said, rubbing her back.

"Yeah and we all know Dreeis crazy ass is dangling on edge normally anyway," she joked, and we both laughed.

"Leave my baby alone okay!" I said, making her smile. I was so happy I could take her mind off what was going on, even if it was just for a second. "Are you hungry?" I asked.

"Yeah I'm starved. The only person eating around here has been my little chubby cheeks over there," she replied, making a funny face at KJ, and he giggled. I got up and made us tacos, and we had rice pudding for dessert.

"That was so good, Morgan. Thank you," Nic said, walking into her and Kendrick's bedroom after putting KJ to bed.

"Anytime," I said, turning on the TV.

"You sure Dreeis doesn't mind you spending the night with me?" she asked.

"What? No, he stays out all night anyway. Plus you’re my best friend, Nic. I wouldn't care how mad he got," I told her, frowning as she started laughing.

"I love you M-Dollas," she said, laying on my shoulder.

"Love you too, Nic Nac."

"Okay, I never approved that nickname, Morgan!"

"Doesn't matter!" I spat, making us both laugh.

We watched Being Mary Jane on Netflix until we fell asleep. I prayed that Kendrick woke up, because I didn't know if Nic could go on without him.

Chapter One: Paris Knight

When I heard Kendrick was hit by a car, I immediately approached Michael, but he assured me he had nothing to do with it. I was so sick without seeing him walk through KB's. Kendrick was like a drug that my body needed, and when I didn't see him or hear his voice, I had withdrawals. I would sneak upstairs into his office just to get a whiff of his cologne, and every time I did, tears would well up in my eyes. I begged God every night to wake my baby up out of that coma, and I hoped he did.

Today, I decided I was going to visit him in the hospital. I had come up there once to see him, and I got his room number because I told one of the nurses that I was his sister, Paris King. When I walked up, I saw Nic sitting in the chair reading. I backed away slowly, cause I wanted no problems with her crazy quiet ass. I knew today would be a success, because I kept track of when Nic came and went.

I pulled up at the hospital and shut off my engine. I hopped out and headed into the hospital. Once I informed the nurses that his "sister" was here, I headed to Kendrick's room. I had no idea why I was so nervous, but I was. I arrived at his room, and almost burst into tears to seeing him lying there like he was dead. I closed the door and walked over to him slowly.

"Kendrick?" I said as if he would respond.

I sat my purse down, and pulled a chair close to the side of his bed. I grabbed his hand in mine, and it felt so good to do so. I could barely touch him for more than ten seconds these days without him snatching away. I kissed the back of his hand, and let my tears fall down my face.

"I miss you, Kendrick. I hope that if you wake up, you will realize that I love you and we belong together. I want you to know I forgive you for moving on and having a kid. I can put that behind us," I said to him, hoping he could hear something.

I smiled at the thought that I could use this chance to kiss his lips. Kendrick had never let me kiss him, ever. It was strictly sex and nothing else. I stood up with his hand still in mine and planted my lips on his. My body got goose bumps all over, at the feeling of his lips against mine for the first time, even with the feeding tube in the way. I instantly got wet. I planted a few more kisses on his soft lips, before sitting down; *if only he could kiss me back*, I thought.

I sat there and talked with him for a little longer before my phone beeped, letting me know Nic would be showing up in about 30 minutes to take up all his damn time! I swear I hated her.

"Well it's time for me to go so that Lolita can come and sit with you for the rest of the day and night, Kendrick." I kissed his lips once more as the nurse walked in and startled me.

"I thought he was your brother?" She asked raising her eyebrow.

"He is. We kiss on the lips in our family. Mind your business," I spat, and quickly rushed out. I prayed that stupid nurse didn't blab about his sister visiting him, because they would immediately know it was my ass who showed up. I sped home feeling happy that Kendrick and I had shared our first kiss.

Chapter Two: Kendon King

I was sick. The longer my brother stayed in that coma, the madder and sadder I got. The disrespect was to the nth degree. I really wanted to know who was behind this shit. We had already killed the niggas who said they were hired on to do the job. Kendreeis and I were now focused on who the fuck hired them. We had a name, but couldn't find the nigga–Houston. His niggas, before we killed they asses, told us Houston ran the drug game up in Chicago, and some other nigga with clearly more brains took over his shit. He decided to pick up and head to Baltimore and take us down, one by one, once he found we ran shit over here.

Kendreeis was coming over so that we could devise a plan on how to catch this nigga. He hadn't been anywhere that we assumed a nigga like him would be. Jessica was at the gym with Nic and Christy, so I invited over Gina. Gina knew any nigga that was a boss, and even the niggas that thought they were bosses–only good thing about having a gold digging hoe around; she'd have that info if you needed.

Kendreeis and I were in my living room when Draco escorted Gina in. She was smiling and switching in a tight ass dress. She made sure to give Dreeis and I full view of her fat ass. She sat down next to me and kissed my cheek.

"Aight, that's not what you here for." I needed to make this quick before Jessica returned.

"Damn okay. So what's up?" she frowned.

"You know a nigga named Houston?" Kendreeis asked, hopping straight to the point.

"Yeah I do. He's some nigga from Chicago that's known for hiring niggas to do his dirty work. In Chicago, he had a reputation for killing a gang of niggas that crossed him, even a couple head honchos. He was on top until some nigga named French took over everything out there, and basically had his ass deported," she chuckled at her last sentence.

"You ever seen him before?" I asked her.

"Yeah, he is never at the places you'd expect, like strip clubs, bars, and shit. He is usually at local cafe's, malls, all shit that's pretty PG," she replied.

"Where have you seen him multiple times? Where does he frequent?" I asked.

"Damn. What this nigga do to y'all?!" she inquired.

"Don't fucking worry about it. Where do you see this nigga a lot?" Kendreeis spat.

She stared daggers through him and rolled her eyes. She smacked her lips, then turned her attention toward me and said, "City cafe, he is usually always there. He does go to strip joints on occasions, but he will have about 30 niggas with him if he does. He never comes to KB, though," she smiled at me.

"City's hunh?" I raised my eyebrow and smiled at Kendreeis. "Well thanks Gina, that was all we needed. We about to head out."

"I gave all that info and I get no dick?!" she pouted and folded her arms.

"Gina, I thought you said we could be homies. You know I have a girl," I pleaded, not having the time or energy to argue and listen to her cry about her undying love for me.

"Okay," she said somberly. She hugged me and stood up. "If you really want to catch him, reach out to his baby mama, Honey. She strips at Vido's. I bet if you could hire her at KB's, he would no doubt show up," she smirked and walked out. We was definitely gon' get up with Honey, but before all that, we were gon' stake out City's.

I called Jules, Maurice, Ricky, and newly promoted Damien. Damien got promoted when Kendrick killed Trenton. Damien was always loyal as fuck and rode for us. We just had no room for him with the big dogs, but when a spot opened up, it was only right to slide him in. I didn't call Kayden, but I told him all that Gina told me, just to put him up on game. I needed him focused on his music and not this shit. He loved it just like us, but I felt if you had some legit shit that you could make money with and loved just as much, do it. As for my brothers and I, the drug game was what we loved and nothing else compared.

"Alright y'all. City's has only two entrances, and sometimes after this nigga does dirt, he enters from the back one for about two weeks," Kendreeis started.

"Bitch ass nigga," Damien chimed in. I laughed cause this little nigga was ready.

"We gon, take shifts staking it out, because we still need to run KB's and make sure our operation is still going as usual. The nigga goes at all times of the day, which is why we need to do this. Jules and Maurice, since y'all pick up the product at 4am, your shift will be 9am to 5pm, just to make sure you're well rested and ate and shit," I chimed in. It was nothing worse than having a sleepy nigga on a stake out.

"Ricky and Damien, y'all got 5pm to 1am because y'all should be done collecting and counting the money by 12pm as usual. That way y'all have time to nap, relax, whatever. Kendon and I will take 1am - 9am, just because King Brothers opens at 2pm and that's where we sometimes double check the money count, make calls, etcetera, and run the place. Plus we not tryna hear Jessica and Morgan's mouth about being gone from 5pm-1am. Is this cool with everybody?" Kendreeis finished.

Everybody nodded, and we continued to plan that shit to a tee. That Houston dude and any niggas he had left was about to feel the wrath like no other.

Chapter Two: Gina Cornell

I was getting so tired of Kendon playing me to the left ever since Jessica came into the picture. Where was this bitch for the past year when I was helping Kendon with everything? Whenever he asked me to do something, I did it with no questions asked. This whole time, I thought I was making an investment into our future together. It's almost like putting money into a business just for someone else to come and say they own it and reap the benefits. As a wise woman once said, you teach a dog how to walk and they'll walk off with another bitch. That's exactly what Kendon was doing to me in this very moment.

Although I messed with his cousins Kayden and Khayman, Kendon was my heart. When I messed with his cousins, it was simply to get some dick, or just because they wanted some pussy and I didn't want to be a party pooper by acting like a bitch. With Kendon, I enjoyed spending time with him and the conversations we would have in bed while smoking a blunt. We never went on dates or anything, but that is not even what I cared about, as long as I could spend time with him.

This shit was just not fair to my girls and I, cause we were the ones that acted as wifey before these power puff girls decided to slide on in. I hated seeing Paris cry herself to sleep over Kendrick, cause I knew she really loved that nigga and bent over backwards for him. So for this muthafucka to just skip over her ass for some moist ass young hoe had me furious.

I was going to meet up with my girls today, just to have a little chitchat and catch up. We needed each other more than ever at this point. We decided to have lunch at the Miss Shirley's on Cold Spring Lane, since Paris and I were off tonight.

"Heyy!" July said, standing up. She no longer worked at KB's because she had a baby now, and her baby daddy Trenton met his maker earlier than expected; and over a bitch.

I hugged her and then Paris before sitting down. "How you been Juju?" I asked July.

"I've been alright, trying to make ends meet. I got a new boo, who has a pretty sufficient income right now, and he helps a lot!" she half smiled.

"New boo? Tell me more?" Paris smiled.

"Well his name is Harley Gary. He's from Chicago, and right now he is just trying to get his hustle up over here so that he can run shit like he did in Chicago," she said, sipping her water the waiter brought.

"Harley? Is his brother named Houston?" I frowned.

"Yeah, they moved here together," she confirmed.

"Why?" Paris quizzed.

"Girl, Kendon and Dreeis is looking for that nigga and I don't know why, so don't ask. However, it sounds like they have a price on his head," I informed them.

"What the fuck?" July frowned. "Are they purposely trying to kill every nigga I get with?" she rolled her eyes.

"Yeah, you better warn him cause you know them Kings catch all their enemies and fast," I told her.

"Why man? It's like I have a curse!" July shook her head.

"Maybe Kendrick has a thing for you and he don't want you with nobody," I joked.

"Bitch I wish!" July laughed as we high fived.

Paris was staring at us, looking mad as hell. "That's not funny, y'all. Plus my boo is in a coma, he ain't even the one looking for that nigga. It's his brothers, so maybe Kendon got a thing for you July!" she said, not taking her eyes off me.

"Whatever hoe!" I said, poofing her from afar.

We put in our drink and food orders, then continued to chat. Paris told us how she visited Kendrick in the hospital by telling the nurses she was his sister. She told us that a nurse walked in on her kissing his lips and became suspicious, making her run out of the hospital. By the time she was done, we were dying laughing.

"Why would you kiss his ass anyway? You know that mouth been between his little girlfriend's legs!" I laughed, and so did July.

"How you know?!" Paris shot back.

"Bitch Kendrick is a fucking freak. I bet he eat ass too!" July said, making me laugh.

"Y'all wouldn't know shit! I'm the only one at this table that has fucked him!" Paris yelled, making a few people at the restaurant look over.

"We don't need to, boo. All the bitches that have fucked him have plenty stories to tell, and they are pretty freaky. One stripper told me she and her homegirl had a threesome with Kendrick, and he put it in every hole possible, then nutted on their faces. She even showed me a handprint he left on her ass from spanking and squeezing that shit!" I said matter of factly, while putting ketchup on my wedges.

"Can y'all shut the fuck up! That don't mean he eating ass and pussy!" Paris yelled loud as fuck.

"Quiet down bitch!" I whispered to her ignorant ass.

"That nigga put a baby in her, he licking every crevice of her body. Accept it and get over it." As soon as July finished, Paris hopped up and walked away.

“You ain’t even met his mama!” I yelled after her delusional ass.

I didn't even try to stop her as she stormed off. She was way too sensitive over that shit. She knew Kendrick was messing with other females, so she can’t be mad about that. Plus, she knew like I knew that Kendrick was serious about old girl if he proposed and got her pregnant. She needed to pull her damn head out of Fool's Paradise, and soon!

Chapter Two: Nic Fuller

Kendrick had been in his coma for what seemed like forever. I stayed in the hospital room with him all day, KJ and I. I started taking an online class, so I would do my assignments in the room with him. I would only go home to shower, clean up the house, turn in my assignments on the Internet, and clean up/feed KJ or let him play with his toys. I was so sad, and I hoped he woke up soon, if at all. The doctor was saying that it didn't look good. I cried at least twice a day when I thought about it.

I got up to go get some ice water with my baby and I heard them yell "Cold Blue! Cold Blue!" over the intercom. I rushed back to the room, and the doctors were in there attempting to resuscitate Kendrick. I covered my mouth to hold in my scream and tears, and KJ started crying like he knew what was happening. After what seemed like ten minutes of non-stop attempts, they finally got his heart beating again.

***

Two more weeks had passed since that flat line, and it happened three more times. I felt like I was going to die every time. I needed my baby to come back. He promised me forever.

KJ was sleep, and I decided to talk to Kendrick like I usually did. I grabbed his lifeless hand in mine.

"Baby it's me, Nic. I need you to come back. Kendrick and I need you bad. I don't like seeing you like this. Kendreeis, Kendon, Jules, Ricky, and Maurice have been hitting the pavement non-stop to find out who did this to you." Tears began to stream.

"Kendrick baby, I miss you so much. I love you. I need you, baby. Remember when you begged me not to leave you? Well now I'm begging you baby, to stay with me. Kendrick, please. You promised me forever," I said, crying and kissing all over his face. Nothing. I cried for 30 more minutes straight.

***

The next morning, I went to buy groceries for the house. As I was putting the bags in the trunk, I heard someone call my name. I turned around to see that Houston guy.

"Hi," I said dryly as I picked Kendrick up out of the basket. *Why was he everywhere I was?*

"Hey, you need some help?"

"No I'm okay. Thank you." I started to put Kendrick in his car seat.

"I heard about your boy," Houston said dryly.

"Yeah well, I hate whoever would take him from his family that needs and loves him. I hope they rot in hell," I said angrily as I buckled KJ in.

"Damn ma. You must really love that nigga," he said smiling. I was irritated, because right now was not a happy smiley ass time for me.

"Yeah I do. Very much." I finished buckling baby Kendrick in, and closed the back door. I headed around to the drivers side.

"Hey if you ever need anything while he's out of commission, let me know. I'm here for you," he said, licking his lips. I know this nigga didn't think I was gon' be busting it open for him while my nigga was in a coma.

"Why?"

"Why what?" he frowned.

"Why will you be there for me? You don't even know me, yet you want to be a shoulder to lean on?" I raised one eyebrow.

He chuckled. "Damn girl, I'm just a nice guy."

"You want some pussy?" I asked straight up, and smiled seductively.

He bucked his eyes and smiled back, biting his lip. "Damn ma, I mean if-"

"Thought so nigga. Well let me save you some time and let you know now that you will not be getting up in this right here. I'd rather ride Kendrick's dick on soft mode while he lay in that coma than let you even see my panties. So scram buddy, and stop sniffing around for scraps like a damn alley cat."

He looked like the scream mask, because his jaw fell open. "Damn ma...I...wa...was just trying to be ni-"

I opened my car door and got in. "Well thanks anyway Houston for the offer, but I'm gonna decline!" I closed my door and drove off.

***

I dropped the groceries off, fed my baby and myself, and cleaned us up. I then headed to the hospital to spend the night.

Chapter Three: Michael Lodenn

When I heard about Kendrick, I had never been happier. Looks like I'm not the only one who wanted that nigga out of the way. It was Thursday, and I knew Nic went grocery shopping every other Thursday. I had been watching her for weeks, but was too scared cause of that nigga Kendrick, I'll admit. I knew he was a hot head and could get reckless, but now that he was out cold and Paris told me she got word that he wasn't gon' wake up, I felt bolder than ever.

I had Apple with me, cause I needed her to take the baby while I had some alone time with Nic. She always had that damn baby with her. Apple wouldn't help in fear of Kendrick, but now that she knew he was out of commission, she was all in.

"Alright there she is," I told Apple as we watched Nic pushing the cart out the store.

"And what the fuck am I supposed to do with the baby?"

"You can take it to her mom's house," I replied without taking my eyes off Nic. She was so beautiful.

"And what's gon' be my excuse for having the baby?" she frowned.

"I don't know, figure some shit out! Let's go!" Damn her ass was annoying.

We hopped out the car and crept up on Nic unknowingly. I grabbed her and threw my keys to Apple, who had already snatched her baby from the shopping cart.

"My baby!" Nic was fighting and squirming.

Apple ran to my car and sped off. I was glad it was kind of dark and Nic parked far. I guess getting exercise wasn't smart for her in this case. I threw her in the passenger side of her car through the driver side, and I slid in after her.

"Michael, what the fuck are you doing!"

She attempted to get out and chase after Apple, but I slapped her hard as hell, making her nose bleed. She looked at me with so much fear and tears in her eyes. I hated to hit her, but she needed to cooperate.

"Are you fucking crazy?!"she yelled, and punched me in my nose hard as hell. *Damn!*

I backhanded her two more times, and banged her head hard on the window, causing her to pass out.

"Finally. Fuck!" I said, out of breath, and cranked up her car.

I sped to my crib and quickly parked. I threw her unconscious ass over my shoulder, and headed to my apartment. Once inside, I tied her wrists to my bed's headboard. Her face was covered in blood from her busted nose, lip, and blood coming from her head onto her face. The sight of her "Mrs. Kendrick King" tattoo disgusted me. I despised that nigga. I poured ice-cold water over her, and she woke up. My heart broke knowing I did this to her, but I had to.

"Where's my baby?" she said in a defeated tone.

"He's at your mothers." Apple had just text me saying she gave the baby to Nic's mom Mariah, and just ran off with no explanation. Dumb bitch.

"Why you doing this, Michael?" she said with tears streaming her face.

I pulled a chair up to my bed, cause it was wet from the water I threw on her. "Cause Nic. I love you and I needed to explain myself."

She exhaled heavily, "Explain what, Michael?! I need to get my baby and go see Kendrick." The mention of his name angered me, and I slapped her hard. She was here with me, thinking of that stupid nigga.

"Ahh!" she screamed and began to cry.

"You love that nigga more than me?!" I yelled, standing with my fists balled up.

"Michael, please stop this!" she yelled through tears. Her teeth were covered in blood from the blows I delivered to her pretty face.

"Nic. Baby. I love you and I want us to be together! Don't you want the same?" I said, kneeling down.

She looked down at me and began to sob hysterically "Michael, I don't love you anymore. I've moved on, and I need you to see that and let me go. I have a family now." She looked so sad that she was here with me, and it hurt me.

"Shut the fuck up bitch!" I yelled, ripping her pants off.

"No Michael! No, don't do this! Kendrick baby, if you can hear me, please wake up!" she yelled, trying to untie her wrists from my bedposts.

"I tried to do it the nice way, but you just can't stop begging for that thug nigga! He ain't gon' never wake up, dumb ass!" I yelled, making her cry. How dare she be calling out for this nigga in my presence! How could she disregard everything we had?

I ripped her shirt open and admired her body. "Since you don't love me no more, I need one more taste!"

"No Michael! No! No!" she yelled, squirming and trying to fight me off, but since she had no hands available, it was hard.

I backhanded her and ripped her panties off. I was going in this pussy raw, and it made me smile. I ate her out for a bit and she didn't cum, which pissed me off. She tried pulling away, but I manhandled her legs open, making her cry harder. Mad as hell, I unbuckled my pants and released my dick. I rammed into her and it was dry as hell. It hurt my feelings. Nic used to be my baby and here I was having to tie her up, beat her, and rape her. I continued to pump into her, and after awhile she wasn't dry.

"Yeah, like that baby," I moaned. Nic had the best pussy ever. I'd only had it once, but the shit was memorable.

She turned her head to the side so she didn't have to look at me and stared at the wall. I sped up and came hard as hell all inside her. I kissed from her stomach to her neck. She laid there as if she was dead. I kissed her swollen lips, and she bit me hard.

"You stupid bitch!" I yelled, slapping her. She didn't scream or cry; she just lightly flinched and laid there, defeated. I untied her roughly, and manhandled her downstairs. It was nighttime, so only a few people were outside. They stared because she had on no bottoms, a ripped open workout top, and a sports bra. Her face was fucked up and her hair was disheveled. I threw her into her car, hopped in, and sped to her house. I dropped her to her mother's house. I unlocked her doors and kicked her out the passenger side onto the lawn. She groaned in pain as I hopped out her car.

"I hate you Nic!" I yelled, and kicked her in the stomach.

I booked it two blocks, and had Apple pick me up. I was done with Nic. All that I'd done for her, and she shitted on me. At least I got some pussy and didn't have to worry about Kendrick coming after me. I smiled at the thought. It quickly faded as I thought about my broken heart.

Chapter Three: Nic Fuller

I was in disbelief at what just happened to me. The timing couldn't have been any worse. Kendrick was in a coma, while Michael was torturing me. I wished so much that Kendrick had killed him when he initially wanted to. I couldn't believe I spared his life. My body was bruised as fuck, and I couldn't move. Blood was all over my inner thighs, and my face was in so much pain.

"Maaaaaaaaaaaa!" I yelled, hoping she heard me. I had no energy to walk to the door.

"Maaaahhhhhh!" I cried and yelled at the same time as I inhaled the scent of the freshly-cut grass. Thank God the porch light turned on and my mom appeared.

"Nic?! Baby?! Oh my Lord! Baby, what happened to you?!"

"Mommy, where is my baby?!" I yelled through tears.

"He's in his crib inside, baby. I been calling you all day...wha...what happened to you?! Where are your clothes?!" My mother was horrified as she looked over my body.

"Michael! He kidnapped me and beat me up! And he raped me, ma!" I cried hard.

My mother was holding my face "Oh baby. I'm gon' kill his ass!" my mother said angrily.

She picked me up as if I was a bride, and carried me inside. She put some shorts on me, and drove me to the hospital. They checked me out, cleaned me up, and gave me some pain medication, stitches in my head, an STD test, and a plan B bill.

"Why didn't you tell them who did this, baby?!" my mom asked, driving me to her house.

"I want to get him myself, ma," I said almost in a whisper, looking out the window and enjoying the blasting heater. She nodded in agreement and continued driving. I couldn't believe Michael, but I was out for blood now. He better watch his back, cause I was gon' kill that nigga.

***

It had been about four days since my incident with Michael. My body was still a bit bruised up, and my face was still sore from all his slaps and punches. My lip was still sore, and I had a bruise and scar under my eye. I refused visits from everyone but my mom, because I knew the girls would tell Kendreeis, Kendon, and Kayden, and I wanted to handle this on my own. At least I thought I did.

***

After the gym, I picked up KJ from my mother. She was telling me that Danielle had been running the streets with some older girls. I already knew that when I saw her ass at KB's with that hoe Paris and some other bitches. After we talked for a bit, I went home and showered, fed KJ and myself, then headed to see Kendrick.

We had been there a couple hours, and I couldn't help myself. I laid in the hospital bed with Kendrick and kissed his lips. I missed him so much and I was so scared without him being awake. I had nightmares every night, thinking someone would break in and kidnap the baby and me. I laid KJ on my chest and we took a catnap.

I woke up to him giggling; my baby always laughed so much. It was hard to be sad around him. I was stunned as I saw Kendrick holding him over us in his bed. I hopped out slightly scared.

"Kendrick?!"

"I woke up about 30 minutes ago, and the nurse took that tube out my mouth," he smirked, and then his smile faded. He was just as sexy as ever, except his once low fade was now a short curly fro.

"Oh my God!" I yelped. I planted kisses all over his face. "I missed you so much. Do you remember anything?" I asked, holding his face.

"What the fuck happened to your face," he asked angrily, ignoring my question. He sat up slowly, wincing in pain while holding onto KJ.

"I uh...uhm…it…" I stuttered as I backed away.

"Close the door, Nic," he said, referring to the hospital door. I did as he asked. "Now, what the hell happened to your face?"

I burst into tears. "Michael. He kidnapped me when you were in a coma. He…he…beat me and raped me, Kendrick," I said, almost in a whisper through tears. His jaw was clenching, and his nostrils flared. He began to laugh out of anger.

"So you telling me that while I was out cold, this nigga put his hands on you and raped you?" he asked rhetorically, then got out the bed and handed me the baby. He snatched off all the wires and things attached to him, making a loud beep go off alerting the nurses. He brushed his teeth, quickly dressed, and flung open the door.

"Let's go!" he yelled over his shoulder as the nurses ran up.

"Mr. King! Mr. King!" the nurses yelled after him.

"He's checking out," I stated the obvious as I rushed after him, holding KJ.

Kendrick sped home with a furious look the whole time. We arrived home, and I put KJ in his crib.

"Do you know where that nigga took you?" he asked.

"His apartment," I said in a low tone. He walked over to me and hugged me tight. He kissed all over my face and then my lips.

"Baby, I'm sorry I wasn't here to protect you. But I promise you nothing will ever happen to you again. Not while I got air in my fucking lungs!" he said with a single tear rolling down his face. "Fuck!" he yelled and rubbed his hand over his face in frustration.

He grabbed my hand and led me to the bathroom, then began to undress me. He kneeled down in front of me, and stared and rubbed over the bruises and cuts he saw.

"Nic. I'm killing this nigga," he said in a calm tone. "Tonight," he said, looking up to see my expression.

He stood up and kissed me some more. He ran us a bath in the Jacuzzi tub, and made sure to use lavender in it. He undressed as I sat on the closed toilet and admired his toffee colored physique. He was beautiful.

"I actually like your new hairdo," I chuckled.

He chuckled too, and checked himself out in the mirror. He was butt naked with the gold chain I bought him on. He really wore it every day, like he said he would. His dick made my mouth water; it had been forever since I'd been with him. He went and got in our huge tub, and I turned up the baby monitor before walking over to join him.

"You're still just as beautiful as ever, even with all these marks that bitch ass nigga put on you." he said, making me blush. He bit his juicy lip, and reached his hand out for me to get in. I sat on the other end and he massaged my feet, which felt so damn good.

"I love you Kendrick. I missed you so much. I been having nightmares every night," I said with tears running down my face.

"I love you too baby girl, and it's okay, I'm here now. Come here," he said.

I slid over to him, and he cuddled me from behind. It felt so good and safe being in his arms in the hot bubble bath. I felt like nothing could touch me when I was with him, and so far, that was proven to be true. I turned towards him and kissed his lips. We kissed hard and passionately. He kissed my neck, then turned my body towards him to suck my nipple.

"Ahhhhh," I moaned out.

"These are beautiful. Perky and plump," he said in between licks and sucks. "You sure you're ready to have sex, babe? We don't have to do anything," he offered. I swear, I loved him more than anything.

I shook my head no. "No babe. I've been missing your touch. I need you inside me. I need you to make me feel better," I pleaded.

He stared into my eyes with his mouth open. He was so adorable. He washed us off and carried me to our bed. He laid me down and planted kisses all over my body. He kissed and licked my stomach until he reached my pussy. He sucked on my clit hard, and put two fingers in me.

"Ahhh Kendriiiick," I moaned. I had tears flowing out of my eyes; I missed him so much.

He continued to lick, suck, and finger me until I came twice. He licked it up and planted soft kisses on it. He climbed on the bed, between my legs, and tongued me down.

"I love you baby girl. You know that, right?" he said in between kisses. I shook my head yes. He entered me and I inhaled heavily. He pinned my hands above my head and stroked my insides. He felt too good, and I knew we belonged together. He licked my tears and planted kisses on my cheeks as he thrusted in and out.

"I missed you, Kendrick." I could say it one hundred times.

Our bodies were so close that it felt like we were about to become one. He sped up a little and that shit was feeling good as hell, making me cum hard.

"Damn ma. Fuck," he moaned into my mouth, and kissed me passionately. He placed his hands under my knees, and raised himself up a bit. He sped up his pace, and all you could hear was him beating my shit up.

"Nic. I swear you got the best shit out here, ma. I love you so fucking much," he said, thrusting in me.

"Kendrick, ah baby I'm cumming again!" I moaned.

"Me too ma. Fuck," he moaned as he went faster and soon exploded.

He continued to stroke me slowly, and then lowered himself to kiss me hard. He kissed my neck and collarbone. He moved my hair out of my face and kissed all over it with his dick still inside me.

"Baby I'm sorry," he said, looking in my eyes. I nodded, saying I understood.

"You still like me even though-?"

"Yes baby girl. Of course. Always and forever. Love you, like you; all that good shit. What he did to you don't change that," he said as he kissed the back of my hands and lips. He flashed his beautiful smile, making me warm all over.

I placed my hands on his face as kissed me passionately. We made love two more times before he got up to handle Michael.

Chapter Three: Kendrick King

I re-showered, brushed my teeth again, and dressed; fresh from a coma to the streets. I was beyond mad. I wanted to go straight from the hospital to this nigga, but I couldn't. One, I needed to send a couple texts to set a few things up. Two, my baby needed me and that was more important. She needed me to hold her, reassure her, and make love to her, and I made sure to do that. My heart was filled with rage. I didn't want to show it too much to Nic, cause I didn't want her to think I was upset with her or anything. My baby was innocent and sweet, and that's what I loved about her, but don't get it twisted– Nic would fuck a bitch up any minute, especially regarding our baby or me. But she was a positive light in my life, where so many negative people and situations surrounded me. She took me on a vacation away from this shit when I was with her.

I was pissed that this nigga disrespected me and then took advantage of her. I don't know what the fuck was going through his mind when he thought he could violate my bitch. I hated that she thought she was damaged goods, and that I wouldn't want her anymore cause of his ass. Why this non street-smart muthafucka attempted to fuck with a nigga of my caliber, I will never understand.

He had to be the stupidest nigga on Earth. Like a fucking fool, he called Apple's name when he threw her is keys; Nic told me. Stupid ass. And he took her to his apartment to commit his crime. I knew where his ass lived, from when I was gon' kill his ass before. I know he acted out thinking I was a goner, but he should've waited until they were lowering me in my grave. I thank God he didn't, though. I had only been out my coma three hours, but I didn't give a fuck!

I got a text on my dummy phone from my cousin on my mother's side, Cinnamon. I had her leave a note on Michael's door that simply said, "I'm woke." She said he looked like he was about to shit bricks. I laughed. Soon as he entered his house, a big buff gay nigga that I had Cinnamon hire tackled him. I texted her back to tell her to spare me the gory details on what came after.

I smirked as I sped to KB's to take care of Apple while them four niggas had a little fun with Michael. That bitch wanted some alone time with me, and she was about to get it. She just better make the best of it, cause it was gon' be her last day on God's green Earth. I was out for blood more than any vampire you'd ever run across. I had never been this angry in my life. I felt like Ted Bundy or some shit, cause I was ready to lay a whole fucking city out over fucking with Nic. Every muthafucka breathing knew I didn't play about my girl, and whoever didn't know was about to find the fuck out.

I walked into KB's, and all the waitresses were hugging me and shit.

"Kendrick, when did you get out?" they asked.

I simply said, "Today," and kept walking through to my office.

Niggas was dapping me up and shit, too. Paris saw me and kissed my cheek. I lightly pushed her off, and she had tears in her eyes.

"I'm good Paris, chill out with the crying. A nigga is better," I half smiled.

I thought about being mean, but she really cared and I kind of appreciated it. I walked past Apple, and she looked as if she saw a ghost. I made sure to wink my eye with a smile. She licked her lips and just as I thought, she followed after me like a little puppy 15 minutes later. When she walked in, I told her to close the door. I could tell she was nervous as hell.

Chapter Four: Apple Sanders

"Come sit down," Kendrick smiled.

I was scared as hell when I saw him walk in the club. Michael assured me he was a goner. I would've never helped that nigga if I had of known he'd wake up. Kendrick was just as fine as before, except he had a short curly fro now. He had on black jeans, a black hoodie, and black low top chucks. He was so sexy and he still made me nervous, which was new for me. I sat down slowly like he'd asked.

"You been missing a nigga?" He bit his lip, and I instantly got wet.

"You know I have," I smiled. His cologne made my nipples hard.

"Meet me at my car. And tell Mena you're sick and leaving for the day. Nothing else."

Before he could finish good, I hopped up and ran out the door to inform Mena, then headed to the parking lot. Once he got in the car with me, he reached over and caressed my thigh. It gave me goose bumps it felt so good. His strong, toffee colored hands; even they were fine. He smirked at me, showing those dimples, and his green eyes sparkled. I saw why Paris was in love with this nigga.

"We gon' chill at my crib. Is that cool?"

I shook my head yes, cause I was too nervous to speak. This nigga was everything! He sped to what I assume was his place. "A Tale of 2 Cities" by J. Cole was blasting the whole way there, and his sugar lemon air freshener made me horny.

"But your fiancée, won't she be mad? Or-"

"You know Apple, after being in that coma, I realized settling down at my age is not that good of an idea." he chuckled, not taking his eyes off the road.

"Well I am happy to hear that," I said, caressing the back of his neck.

We arrived at this gated condo community, and he drove to his condo. This shit was decked the fuck out.

"Nice, Kendrick," was all I said as I walked through the door.

He didn't respond; he just grabbed my hand. He guided me to the couch and we sat down. He looked at me and flashed his pearly whites. I almost came just looking at him.

"Apple, you seem like a sweet girl," he said, rubbing his hand up my thick thigh, causing me to tense up. He bit his lip as he did it.

Now y'all, like I said before, no nigga made Apple Sanders nervous. I don't know what it was about Kendrick, and it wasn't like I hadn't fucked with boss niggas before, but chilling with, or fucking a King brother was every bitch's dream, so maybe that's why. All I know is I couldn't wait to feel him inside me.

"Calm down ma. I do bite, though," he winked and smiled, making his dimples appear. Fine ass.

"I am calm." I lied.

He stood up to pour us a drink from the bar. *It's now or never Apple*, I told myself. I walked behind him and ran my hand up his back. He turned around smiling, and then backhanded me to the floor. My nose busted immediately.

"Ah!" I yelped.

I looked up, and he had wrath written all over his face. I knew I had fucked up. I immediately thought of the Thriller video, when MJ turned into that zombie; yeah, I was that scared. I don't know why I went against a nigga like Kendrick, with a bitch ass nigga like Michael.

"You must be the dumbest hoe alive! You helped some nigga kidnap my family? Fuck is wrong with you? You know who the fuck I am!" he yelled, frowning as I stood up. He slapped the shit out of me again, and I fell on the couch.

"Kendrick, please! I'm sorry! I'll do whatever you want, baby!" I tried to plead. He sipped his drink and laughed.

"I thought you liked me, Apple?" he asked, moving his hand from my neck down to my breasts.

"I do, Kendrick! Please. Whatever you want. I'll do it!" I smiled seductively, and tried wiping the blood from my nose with a nearby tissue. He took his liquor to the head, not taking his eyes off me.

"Strip," he said sternly, leaning on his bar. I stood up and began to take my clothes off. He stopped me and turned on "Na Na" by Trey Songz. "Continue," he said, pouring himself another glass of Hennessey.

I began dancing seductively to the song, using all my moves that made me the queen of King of Diamonds, making my ass clap and everything. He had a pole that came up from the floor; this nigga really loved strippers. I twirled on it ass naked all the way down to the floor. He watched me closely, not missing a move, which made me smile. He finished his drink, and folded his arms as he watched me. I continued to fuck it up. He checked his phone, and then abruptly turned off the song with the remote. He walked over to me on the ground, and shoved a one-dollar bill in my mouth while smiling. I just knew I was about to suck his dick. I licked my lips, while looking up at him.

He chuckled, then retrieved his gun from his waist and forced it in my mouth. "Any last words?" he asked, taking his last sip to head

He let off the gun before I could answer.

Chapter Four: Kendrick King

I called the clean-up crew to come and scoop Apple's ass up, and clean any staining. I had to prolong her death until Cinnamon let me know them dudes was done with Michael. That was not something I wanted to see. Apple had some moves on her, too bad she was a dumb hoe, cause she could've brought in big money at KB's.

I sped to Michael's crib since Cinnamon texted and said he was ready for me. I had the windows down, and was smoking some of that new Van Gogh shit we were selling. Damn. I was bumping "Make It Home" by August Alsina, and I was so high I felt like I sounded just like that nigga when I was singing along.

When I got there, I opened the door and saw Michael crying like a bitch. Cinnamon said her homie Vick, and three of his friends had ran up in that a couple times. They tied his ass up to a chair when they were done and left him there with her.

"What's up cousin?" she greeted me.

"What's up?" We hugged, and I walked up and pulled a chair in front of Michael. "So you like raping girls, hunh? Well you raped the wrong one, nigga. How does it feel?" I spat.

"Kendrick man, why you have to do me like that?!" he cried.

I laughed so loud at the audacity of this little bitch. "Nigga, are you crazy?"

"You sent them niggas to ruin me! To take my manhood!" he yelled, with bloody snot running from his nose.

I turned my lip up in disgust. "Shut yo ugly ass up with that crying, my nigga!" I yelled, making Cinnamon laugh. "I warned your bitch ass on several fucking occasions not to fuck with Nic, and you just couldn't take a fucking hint! What, you thought I was just talking, nigga?!" I slapped him with the gun and untied his ass. "Defend yourself, you little bitch!" I yelled, punching the shit out of him and making him fall out the chair. I started whooping his ass, just like he did to Nic. I must've been fucking him up bad, because Cinnamon called my name for me to stop.

"Can't even fight for yourself, you lil pussy nigga. I don't even need a gun for your punk ass," I spat.

"Come on, you can do it! Be a big boy, just like when you was able to take four of them 10-inch dicks back to back up that ass 30 minutes ago, boo," Cinnamon teased, filing her fingernails.

"Ugh Cinnamon. Spare me," I chuckled.

***

We drove his ass to the warehouse, and I poured gasoline on him. He tried to run out, but I knocked his ass to the floor with my gun.

"Fuck! Haven't you done enough!?" he yelled.

"Nigga who the fuck you yelling at?" I said, balling up my gun-less hand.

His bitch ass lowered his voice. "I'm sorry man, don't do this. Come on man I don't know what..."

"You rambling, bitch," I said, nodding my head at Cinnamon.

She lit a match and threw it on his ass. He tried rolling around and shit, but it didn't work. After a couple minutes of him screaming and squirming, we dumped water on him and I emptied eight shots in between his eyes.

After the clean-up crew took care of him, I felt slightly better. Slightly because I got revenge on behalf of my baby, but I still hated that this happened to her. I dropped Cinnamon off at my parent's house, then headed home.

I walked into our bedroom, and Nic and KJ were watching TV. "You got him staying up late with you?" I asked, removing my pullover.

"KJ, tell daddy you're just a night owl like me," Nic replied while cuddling him between her legs.

"Da-ddy," he cooed. I was shocked.

"What you say, little man?"

"Da-ddy! Da-ddy! Da-ddy!" he said excitedly, moving and reaching for me.

I snatched him up and kissed his cheeks. He smelled like that oatmeal bath wash we used on him. "Daddy loves you man," I said, kissing him as he laughed.

I handed him back to Nic, who was smiling, and I went to shower. Once out, I climbed in bed with them and kissed Nic's lips long and hard. "I love you, Nic," I said, looking over at her and kissing the back of her hand.

"I love you more, Kendrick."

I planted a kiss on her neck and shoulder, which smelled so good, then watched cartoons with them all night, like I hadn't just been on a small killing spree. Next on my list was that bitch ass nigga Houston my brothers hit me about. No pun intended.

Chapter Four: Houston Gary

This shit is getting crazy. I'm Houston Gary, and I'm originally from Chi town, where I ran shit over there. I was like Hitler or Joseph Stalin to them muthafuckas. It all changed when I let this snake ass nigga named French into my circle. I groomed his old ass, thinking I found an accomplice and someone to help make my empire bigger and better. Little did I know, this nigga was plotting on me from jump. He got all my niggas and muscle to turn against me. It got to a point where everywhere I looked or went, niggas was blowing bullets my way. I couldn't believe how this nigga took me down. One day French told me to get out of town and never return, or he was gon' blow my brains out. I had a little girl and girlfriend at the time, but shit, I wasn't dying for no fucking body.

I skipped town as soon as possible and ended up in Baltimore. I kept my ear to the streets, and found the drug game was dominated by the King Brothers. I hung around to find out each one of their names, and how much influence they had. I found Kendrick King was the head of the shit, so I wanted him out first. I figured if I killed him, the shit would crumble and it would be easy to take out the rest of the crew. I, of course, had sent some of the little niggas I recruited while out here to kill the nigga. I wasn't gon' do it myself and risk getting killed by his crew, or his father and uncle. I knew his father Kairio and uncle Kylin were ruthless. Killing their son and nephew would wake a sleeping bear, and I didn't want that bear coming after me.

Just my luck, the niggas hit him with the car and didn't even kill him. I heard he was in a coma and hoped his people pulled the plug on his ass. Then, as if I had a lucky charm in my pocket, his bitch ass brothers caught my staff up and them niggas blabbed on me, like the bitch's I had a feeling they were! I almost shit on myself when my brother told me the King family was after me. He was fucking some bitch named July, and she told him her home girl said them niggas was looking for me. I stopped going to all my usual places and laid low at my crib for a bit. I hated them niggas, especially Kendrick- and to make it worse, I wanted his bitch.

I had a girl back in the Chi who had moved here named Honey, but she wasn't Nic. Nic was beautiful as fuck, and I had to have her. That nigga Kendrick lucked up, cause every nigga wanted that one bad bitch that hadn't been passed around. If she was bad as fuck, usually a couple hustlers and shit had hit. I had never seen the chick before, so I knew she was a good one. That nigga had her nose wide open, cause I thought once he was in that coma, she'd be ready for some new dick. But nah, she wasn't fucking with a nigga. She wanted that old sleeping beauty ass muthafucka.

BOOM! BOOM! BOOM!

I jumped when I heard somebody banging on my door, spilling my beer in my lap. I grabbed my gun and quietly looked through the peephole to see it was my brother Harley. I smacked my lips and opened the door.

"Damn man, you scared the shit out of me! Why the fuck you knocking like the police!!?!!" I said, letting him in while looking at the wet spot on my crotch.

"Nigga we need to get a game plan or get the fuck out of dodge! We fucked with the wrong people, my nigga!" he said, pacing.

"What you mean?! What happened now?!" I asked, worried like a muthafucka.

"Well for one, Kendrick woke up and that nigga is gunning for you. Secondly, his father Kairio and uncle Kylin is looking for your ass too, and three, they killing all the niggas we put on, nigga!" he yelled loud as hell, with his scary ass.

"Okay relax. Who we got left?! Get them over here!" I said frantically.

"We had six niggas total, but the three you sent to rob they trap house got decapitated!!" he damn near screamed. These niggas was gruesome with they shit. My lip turned up at the thought.

"Fuck!!! At least they brought me the product and money they were able to get," I smirked, looking at my brother who was clearly not in the joking mood. "Well call them nigga! The fuck you waiting on!!!" I yelled, irritated by him.

Harley started calling them over so we could make a plan. Those King niggas had killed over 30 niggas looking for me, and I was scared as hell. I just knew 30 of us could take them down easy, but I guess not. They were literally spraying my niggas with bullets at all times of the day. They had niggas everywhere, and what was so bad was that you didn't know who was working for them and who wasn't. It was like Russian roulette. If all else failed, I was gon' snatch up my brother and skip town on everybody. I'd have to get up with Honey and my daughter another time.

***

"Alright y'all, we need to figure something out because the job was not done. Well it was done, but not correctly," I started.

I called a meeting with the little amount of niggas I had left. I was fronting like a muthafucka for they asses. I was acting all tough and shit, like I wasn't sweating the King family looking for me, but a nigga was about to shit bricks at every thump and bump in the night. You couldn't burp around me without me flinching. They were retaliating so crucially that it wasn't even a good idea for us to walk to the corner store. When you came out, you may get some bullets deposited.

"So what's the plan, boss?" one of my niggas named Kip asked.

"Is there any way for y'all to find and run up on any one of the brothers? If so, we can just do that and shoot one of them. We don't really have any room for too much planning, y'all," I blurted.

"Nigga what? Are you crazy? As soon as we run up, we getting shot at!" my brother Harley yelled. "These are not no amateurs that we fucking with, Houston!"

"Well where the fuck are your ideas nigga, since you so fucking smart!" I yelled.

"I don't have any, but I also told you that coming here to Baltimore to fuck with these niggas was not a good idea!" he frowned.

This nigga was pissing me off. One, because he did warn me and two, we was in some deep shit and I had no idea how to get out, other than skipping town like a bitch. I looked over and saw Gordon, Kip, and Larry staring at us like we had lost our minds. I knew they were thinking that we was some weak niggas, and I needed to save face fast.

"So, I'm gon' do some thinking tonight and get at y'all later," I finally said.

"Man, I don't know how much time we got. These niggas got people everywhere and are taking no prisoners!" Larry yelled, frustrated.

"Well I'm in charge nigga, and I said I need to fucking think on it!" I spat, balling up my fists.

"Nigga you approached me like you had a solid plan to come up off these King niggas, and now you ain't got shit!" Larry yelled back.

"Are you trying to lose your life talking to me like that, little nigga?" I yelled, moving closer to him.

He stood up out of his chair as I got closer, and laughed at me while looking me up and down. "Nigga I heard about your style back over in Chicago. You all bark and no muthafucking bite!"

"Well what you heard was bullshit! Now get the fuck out my shit until I hit y'all asses up with my plan!" I yelled, tipping the other guys' chairs up to make them leave. Larry had me fucked up trying to embarrass me like that in front of everybody, and I hoped Kendrick and his people caught up with his ass and killed him. When they finally left, I called my baby mama Honey to let her know where I was gon' be staying at, in case I needed to see my daughter.

Chapter Five: Christy Franks

I was in Vegas with Kayden for a show he had at Tao during the day club. I had gotten a fake ID so that I could enter. Afterwards, we decided to walk the strip, talk, and enjoy the scenery. We stopped by the Coca Cola shop and decided to taste the coca cola's from all over the world.

"This one is nasty as fuck!" Kayden yelped, causing me to burst into laughter.

As I was reading the description of the next drink, I saw him looking past me with a stern facial expression. I turned to see that hoe Gina, and she waved seductively. I was about to get up, but Kayden stopped me.

"Chill ma. She not worth it. I'm yours." I knew Kayden didn't think I knew he used to fuck her back in the day. Jessica told me that they used to run trains on her fonkey ass.

We finally left the Coke place, because Kayden saw I was irritated. We went to eat at Friday's, and I was still a little upset. I trusted Kayden, and that little shit at the Coca Cola shop pissed me off. I left Trenton for a reason, and one of them wasn't to hop into another relationship where I had to fight bitches off again.

"Christyyyyy, chill ma. Gina is a hoe like that. She gon' act that way with any man," he pleaded, grabbing my hand. I ignored him and sipped my drink. "You so pretty when you mad," he joked, cracking himself up. He got up and decided to sit on the same side of the booth that I was on. I scooted over to not be so close.

"Christy, talk to me. Why you acting out?!"

"Because I know you used to fuck on her, Kayden!" He smiled at me, obviously amused by my anger. "Fuck you smiling at, nigga!?" I spat.

"Yeah, I did used to fuck her, but so did half of us. She and her friends were convenient pussy at the time when we was young hustlers. We would invite them to the crib and basically fuck whichever one of them we wanted. That was it. I haven't smashed in over two years," he said. I rolled my eyes and he turned my face towards him and kissed my lips. "Don't be mad, babe. Don't let that hoe cause friction between us. That's what she wants."

I thought about what he said, and he was right. She would love for me to push Kayden away, right into her loose pussy. We ate and had a good time for the rest of the dinner. We arrived to the hotel and decided to cuddle up and watch some movies. I loved him. He always made me happy, and he treated me so good–so good that when I found out Trenton died, I didn't flinch.

His phone rang and he checked it. "I got to go handle something real quick."

Before I could protest, he ran to the bathroom. I unlocked his phone and read the text from Gina saying she was in her hotel room. My stomach dropped and my heart literally ached. I hurried and put his phone back in place when he came out.

"What kind of business is it?" I asked.

"Nothing much, just need to knock some things out," he said.

Knock some pussy out, I thought. "Let me come," I smirked.

He froze while putting his shirt on. "Nah, it's not a good idea for you to come," he replied.

"And why not?"

"Because there is no need. I'm gon' be in and out. I'll be back before you know it."

In and out I bet, I thought. "Kayden if you don't let me come, I'll be gone when you come back, and I don't want you to ever contact me!" I spat.

He paused, "Fine! Get yo bratty ass up and get dressed!!" he yelled, mad as hell. Surprised, I paused then hopped up and put my clothes on. "Nah, take off that bright top. Black only." I did as he asked.

We headed out, and I noticed he had a gun clipped to his waist. I was starting to regret coming. We got in the car and he opened the glove compartment, and handed me a small cute little gun.

"Awwww, this is so cute!" I beamed.

He just glared at me, wiping the smile off my face. "This thing is for protection. You wanted to come, now you gon' have to man the fuck up." I shook my head yes, and he cranked the car.

We arrived at Treasure Island hotel, which was hella close to our hotel room at the Venetian. He parked and he pulled out his phone. I saw him text Gina that he was here. He shouldn't have gave me this gun, cause if she pissed me off, I may kill her ass. We walked through the hotel, looking normal as possible. We pulled our masks on secretly and got on the elevator. We arrived on her floor, and he knocked.

"Get behind me so she don't see you," he whispered, exposing his face for her.

I hid behind him and we heard Gina look through the peephole. As soon as she opened the door, Kayden and I rushed her with our masks down.

"Close the door!" he yelled to me. I did so, and chuckled cause this bitch had on lace panties, matching bra, and garters. She was ready to fuck him knowing he had a bitch, but I had to give it to her, she was thick as fuck.

"Kayden, what the fuck baby?!" Gina cried out.

Kayden shot me a look to say don't act reckless over that baby shit. I rolled my eyes and plopped down on the bed.

"Gina, you been running your mouth and now you have to pay for it. You told that bitch July we was looking for Houston, and now this nigga knows to hide."

When I heard Houston's name I bucked my eyes. That was the nigga who was on Nic.

"I didn't know it was a secret!" she yelled.

"Lower your muthafucking voice before I kill you early!!!" My pussy got wet watching him. I had no idea Kayden was a thug like the rest, but then again, his last name was King.

"What else you know? If it's good info, I'll let you live!" he said, pointing his gun at her.

"His address that he lays low at is 8553 Grove Lane, Baltimore, MD," she ran off.

"Anything else?"

"His baby mama works at Vido's Girls, and her name is Honey. He tells her everything. His brother Harley frequents Vido's too!" she cried. I couldn't stand her ugly ass. Bitch.

"Thanks," Kayden said as he put his silencer on and killed that hoe. "Let's go, Christy," he said, storming out. I ran and slapped her with my little ass gun. "Christy! Come on!"

We left the hotel and got to our room. We undressed and fucked for hours.

"Ahhhhhh daddy! Fuck this pussy!" I yelled. I was throwing it back like a muthafucka. I had came three times already, and my inner thighs were soaked.

"Damn daddy!" I moaned.

"Damn Christy," he moaned as he tightened his grip on my waist and plowed into me. We both released together and collapsed.

"I love you, Kayden King," I said, out of breath.

"I love you too, Christy King."

"King?"

"Yeah, King."

We decided to shower together, get dressed, and get married by one of those Elvis impersonators. I was finally Mrs. King.

Chapter Five: Kendreeis King

When my brother woke up, I was happy as hell, but we still needed to find that Houston nigga. He hadn't been to City Cafe at fucking all. We finally found out why, when Kayden let us know that Gina blabbed to July, who is currently fucking Houston's brother. I was happy he offed her ass, but then again, we didn't want him doing this shit. It ran through his blood though, and I know he couldn't help it.

We busted up in the address she supplied Kayden with, and the nigga had cleaned his shit out and bounced. His baby mama Honey was still in town, so we knew he was. We knew that anywhere he went, she would know or be following him soon. We arrived to Vido's where she stripped, so that we could pump her for some info.

"Damn," Kendon mumbled, speaking for all of us as we watched her set. She was fucking it up to "Be Real" by Kid Ink and Dej Loaf.

Honey was bad as hell. She was thick as fuck; big ass titties, fattest ass ever, and a beautiful face. I don't know how she ended up with a fuck nigga like Houston. She had a long blonde weave in her head, and honey colored hazel eyes. I'm guessing that's how she got her name. She reminded be of Beyoncé.

"Calm down nigga, we here for business," Kendrick spat with a smile while watching. This nigga Kendrick loved him some strippers. I was surprised as fuck when he settled down with a girl that was actual wifey material, cause he had me worried for awhile. I just knew he was gon' wife a stripper. I shook my head and laughed at my thoughts.

We talked to the owner to have Honey sent to our private lounge area. We sat and waited until she finally walked in. She had on a thong and nothing else. *Gooooooot damn*!

"Y'all been looking for me?" she asked, standing there looking like a tall glass of water, and my brothers and I were definitely parched. It wasn't worth it all, though. I knew what I had at home, and wasn't about to lose that for a quick nut.

"Yeah, sit," Kendrick said sternly. Kendon stared her down with lust in his eyes. He was on the thinnest ice possible with Jessica, and knew his ass shouldn't have been thinking about doing anything.

"We been looking for your baby daddy, and we need your help finding him," I said, getting to business.

"And why would I help y'all?" she frowned her pretty face.

"Because your baby daddy can't protect you, and if you don't comply, we killing you and your daughter," Kendrick spat. I know he wasn't gon' kill the daughter, but we'd def kill her ass.

She stared at him for a moment and licked her lips. "Only cause you sexy," she smirked. Kendrick smiled at her compliment. This nigga.

"Well?" I asked, interrupting her and Kendrick's lustful stare off.

"He's been laying low at his cousin's house. He's planning on kidnapping your girl Nicky, or something like that. He wants her," she ran off.

"Her name is Nic," Kendrick corrected her. "And I wish this nigga would touch my bitch." Honey frowned at his statement, obviously jealous. I laughed.

"What's the address of the cousin?" I asked. I looked at Kendon, and knew this nigga was quiet due to all his lustful thoughts of her. I shook my head and wrote down the address.

"Now call him and make sure he there," Kendrick ordered.

She called him, and he told her he'd be home to his cousins in two hours. We all got up to leave, and she stopped Kendrick.

"We already in the private room. You don't want a show?" she smiled seductively.

"I saw your show," he replied, cheesing like a Cheshire cat.

"No, but I want to give you a different show," she said, dropping her panties. Typical thot. Kendrick admired her body, chuckled, and exhaled heavily like he was begging God to help him.

"Put your clothes on, baby girl. I got what I need at home, so I'm gon' pass," he finally said, patting her on the shoulder, and walking out. She looked dumb as hell and we all wanted to laugh, but held it in for her sake.

Chapter Five: Honey Harris

I'm Honey Harris and I'm a badass bitch. I'm originally from Miami, FL, where I got my start at King of Diamonds, but having to follow my scary ass baby daddy around got me all the way in Chicago, then Baltimore.

I met Houston back in Florida when he came to KOD one night. He was super sexy and seemed to be a boss ass nigga. He stayed flossing and talking big shit, like he was that nigga. Soon as I saw him, I knew I had to fuck with him. We started fucking with each other hard, and then next thing you know, I was pregnant with our baby girl Reagan. She was so beautiful and looked just like her daddy. Unfortunately, after I had her was when I saw that the nigga I was fucking with was not the nigga I was actually fucking with. Houston Gary was a fraud, straight up.

I first realized it when some niggas came beating on my fucking front door, pressing me about him. I threatened them, saying my nigga was gon' fuck they ass up when he found out they was beating on my door and disrespecting me. Soon as Houston came home, way later that night, I let him know that some niggas came looking for him and disrespected me by calling me out my name. I expected my man and baby daddy to hop out the bed and cock his gun to put a bullet in these niggas, but no. What did he do? Nigga had us move to a new state in order to avoid them niggas' wrath.

We moved to Chicago, and I decided to stick by the nigga because he came up quick out there. He was actually running shit in Chi-town, and the cash flow was heavenly. I had everything I wanted, so who cared if my nigga was a fraud? Surely not I. What I soon learned was there are two types of frauds, smart ones and dumb ones; Houston was the latter. He decided to partner up with some old ass nigga named French, and the nigga ended up taking over Houston's empire from the inside out. Next thing you know, I woke up to a text saying that he had moved to Baltimore. I followed him here, but as far as our relationship? That had ran its course. So hell yeah I was gon' help fine ass Kendrick and his brother's take his bitch ass down.

Kendrick was bomb as hell and from experience, I could tell he was not a fraud whatsoever. I wanted him in my life and he, needed me whether he knew it or not. I asked a couple fellow strippers out here about him and they gave me the scoop, letting me know there was a line around the corner for he and his brothers. They told me he had a fiancée' and baby mama, which he did confirm for me. They also told me about some bitch named Paris that was crazy about the nigga. I didn't give a fuck, because I was prepared to cut that long line anyway.

My phone buzzed while I was in the locker room, and I saw it was Houston calling me. "What's up?" I answered, hoping it was to tell me he was home.

"What you doing?" he asked.

"I'm leaving work about to go get Reagan from Casey," I informed him. Casey was my girl who happened to live in Balti. Thank God I had someone.

"Am I gon' see you later?" he asked, and I could tell he was smiling.

This nigga was always trying to get some pussy, and it was not gon' happen. "Yeah, that's why I asked when you would be home," I told him to make sure I didn't ruffle Kendrick's plan.

"Cool ma. Can't wait to be in that stomach," he laughed. I wanted to throw up. It was bad enough that I had let him fuck period.

"Me either boo," I said before immediately hanging up. I prayed that Kendrick and his brothers got this nigga, cause I was tired of hopping towns so Reagan could see him. It'd be easier to just tell her daddy had passed.

Chapter Five: Kendrick King

I left Honey's hoe ass standing there looking dumb. I wish I had met her before Nic though, cause I would've bent that ass right over that lounge couch and went to work. Strippers were a former weakness of mine. My dick got slightly hard at my thoughts. She was bad as hell, no doubt, but I was not about to mess up again. One, I didn't want to hurt Nic again. She was so broken when I cheated that one time that it hurt me too. I love her so much, and to know I made her feel that way was fucking horrible. Secondly, I'm 100% sure she would leave my ass and there would be nothing I could say to make her stay. Third, it all around just wasn't worth it. What was a quick nut gon' do for me? And I'm sure the pussy wasn't as good as my baby girls.

"Kendrick!" I turned around to see Paris. What the fuck was she doing here? I didn't say anything; I just gave a look telling her to spit it out.

"Gina went to Vegas and she never came back!" she said, looking up at me sad as hell.

"Okay?"

"Okay? I think something happened to her!"

"And, you want me to do what?" I raised my brow, irritated.

"I don't know. Maybe find out who did it."

"Or I can keep it pushing. Gina loved the fast life. For all we know, she could've met some nigga and ran off with him," I said nonchalantly.

"Yeah…" she looked down. "What you doing later?" she asked, trying to flirt.

"Bye P," I said, walking to my car.

These hoes were so disrespectful. They clearly saw my brothers and I were taken, but they was still offering it up. And they wonder why we skipped over they ass to be with other chicks that respected themselves too much to be trying to fuck a taken nigga. I was driving home and couldn't wait to get home to my two babies. Soon as Honey hit my phone, we was heading out to Houston's cousins crib.

I pulled into my driveway and made sure the gates were locked. Ever since Honey said Houston wanted Nic, it was constantly on my mind that he would send some reckless nigga to get her. I came in and I smelled enchiladas and baked barbecue beans. My stomach growled loud as hell. I heard Nic talking to KJ, and him laughing. I sighed out of relief, glad that no one had tried anything and she was still here. I walked into the kitchen and sat at the island.

"Look who that is, baby!" Nic said to KJ as she put the pan of enchiladas on the counter. He was giggling as usual in his high chair, and his green eyes lit up, making me smile.

"You haven't cut your hair, I see," she said walking up to me, kissing my lips, and running her hands over my fro.

"I thought you was feeling it?" I joked.

"I am. It gives you a rough sexy look," she smirked seductively. Damn she was fine.

"You ready to eat?" she asked.

"Born," I replied.

I stared at her as she made my plate. She had on pajama shorts and the matching crop top, exposing her toned stomach and sexy belly button ring. She reached into the cabinet for a plate, and I saw the bottom of her small, round, and plump butt, making my dick hard. The baby made her ass fatter and hips a little wider. I was fucking her 25/8. Some days she couldn't even walk regular.

"Why you wearing that in front of me?" I half joked.

"Pajamas?!" she frowned.

"Them ain't no regular pajamas, ma," I said.

She had no bra on, so I saw her hard nipples and piercings; my mouth was watering. A nigga could barely concentrate.

"They're not?" she smiled. Damn she was beautiful; I don't know how I ever cheated.

"Hell nah! I can't eat with you looking like that, my dick hard already. You say you not ready for baby #2, but you wearing shit that make me wanna fuck the shit out you 24/7!" I chuckled, although serious.

"I will put on a robe then, Mr. King," she laughed, bringing me my plate and drink.

"Nah no need. What's for dessert?"

"Homemade German chocolate cake. And me," she smiled seductively. I wanted to get straight to dessert.

We ate our food and after she put the baby to sleep, she came in the room.

"Come here," I told her as she closed the door. She walked over to me, laying on the bed, and straddled me. I put my hands on her small waist. "You know a nigga named Houston?" I questioned.

"Yeah, he's a nice guy," she replied.

"How so?"

"He offered to help me out while you were in a coma," she said. I immediately got pissed that he was that close to her. Making conversation and shit.

"I don't want you talking to other niggas right now, ma."

"What you mean?" she frowned.

"What's going on?"

"That nigga Houston wants you. He's planning to kidnap you, so I need you to not leave the crib for a while. I might stay at my condo for nights at a time, just because I don't want them knowing where we live. Don't leave this house for the next week. If you need anything, hit me and I will get it for you."

I needed her to be safe in case we didn't catch this nigga tonight. He was known for getting word that niggas knew his whereabouts and dipping. She climbed off me, obviously upset. "You mad?" I asked, frowning.

"You gonna stay at your condo for the rest of the week? The one you used to bring hoes to?" she asked, looking straight ahead.

I exhaled, irritated. "Nic, the last thing on my mind is bringing hoes to my condo. I'm tryna catch this nigga and protect you from him. If you don't leave, he can't follow you home, and if someone is following me in order to get you, it will lead to the condo," I pleaded.

She got up. "I'm gonna go to the guest room."

I hopped out the bed and grabbed her. "Nic, you have to trust me. I'm not doing this to fuck around on you. This some real shit!"

"Then take me with you to the condo!" she said, raising her eyebrow like she caught me up.

"No Nic, that defeats the purpose! I might as well stay here if that's the case!" I knew she said that cause she thought I was gon' cheat. This shit was annoying me.

"The baby and I will go stay with my mother."

She was pissing me off, and I needed to put my foot down. "Nic, this is not a fucking discussion. You gon' stay yo ass here and not leave until I tell you it's safe! Now close the damn door and bring your ass back to bed with me. When I tell you to do something, you need to do it! Not battle me on my decisions. This conversation is over! And fix your fucking face!" I yelled, walking back to the bed.

She closed the door and laid down under the covers. I got in the bed and cuddled up behind her. She moved my hands from her body.

"Why don't you go to your condo now?" she spat.

"Nic, you have to trust me that I'm not doing this to live like a bachelor," I said, hugging her from behind again.

"I trusted you the first time, and you fucked another bitch as soon as you hadn't had any for a couple weeks," she removed my hands again.

"Well why the fuck did you take me back if you was still gon' be stuck on this shit? I'm not gon' be with you if you can't move the fuck on! I can keep it pushing!" I yelled, irritated as fuck.

"Well I'll just go fuck another nigga and we can see how fast you get over that shit!" she spat.

"Aight. Fuck you, Nic!" I wanted to choke her ass, but I was brought up not to hit women; well, my woman. As Suga Free put it, "Never hit a woman, but I'll slap the shit out of a bitch!" Nic was making it hard as hell, though.

I gave up and turned the TV on to wait for Honey's text. Thirty minutes later, she texted me that Houston said he was home. Game time. I hopped up and got dressed. When I came from the bathroom, I heard Nic crying quietly. I didn't give a fuck.

"Where you going?" she asked as she watched me put on my shoes.

"You worry about the nigga you gon' fuck and where he going!" was all I said before I bounced. If she couldn't trust me, then I didn't know what the fuck to tell her.

***

My brothers and I arrived to Houston's cousins crib, and I had to silence my phone cause Nic was blowing me up with texts and calls, asking me where I was and saying sorry. I saw the car that Honey said was his and smiled. We all got out and went around back. Honey gave us all the fucking info. I saw them niggas playing dominoes through the window of a door that Honey told us was broken. Dumb asses. I quietly reached through the broken window and unlocked the door, as Kendreeis and Kendon stayed behind me with their guns ready and loaded. We rushed through the door, and Kendon immediately put a bullet in the cousin's shoulder. None of them had their heat on them. We forced them niggas to the car and drove them to our basement warehouse. We tied them to the chairs and poured gasoline on they ass.

"Who else is helping you?!" Kendreeis yelled to Harley.

"I…I'm no-"

POW!

Before he could finish, I pumped two in his dome. "Now he took too fucking long. Houston, who was helping y'all?" I asked.

His face was bloody and beat the fuck up, thanks to Kendon. I don't know why these niggas chose to run the streets, when they had no hands. Sometimes that would be all you had.

"Just three others. Y'all killed everybody else. Gordon, Kip, and Larry," he ran off.

"Who was in on you kidnapping my bitch?!"

"Just them three. Please my nigga, if you let me live, I will leave and never come back!" his bitch ass pleaded. I laughed, and then went to his cousin.

"What you know?!" Kendon asked, basically reading my mind.

"I was just giving a place to stay. I do-"

POW! POW!

Kendreeis killed his ass. "Useless," he commented after.

"Now nigga, you get it the worst." I lit a match and threw it in Houston's lap.

We all sat and watched him squirm and scream out. Once his squirms and screams stopped, we threw water on him to stop the flames.

"Ugh! What the fuck!" Kendreeis yelled. He always had a weak stomach for this shit. I laughed and called the clean-up crew.

***

When I got home, Nic and KJ were gone. I was too tired to deal with that shit, and took my ass to bed.

I woke up at 8am after hearing my alarm. I showered, brushed my teeth, dressed, and sprayed my everyday cologne. I hopped in my car and headed to her mother's place. I knocked on the door loud as hell. Nic's lil fast ass cousin answered the door.

"Hi Kendrick!" she smiled, cocking her head and licking her lips.

I ignored her and ran up the stairs to Nic's room. She was sleep and had KJ in the crib she bought to have here. I yanked the covers off her ass, causing her to wake up.

"Kendrick, what the fuck!"

"Let's go! Get yo ass up!" I yelled. I was mad as hell.

"I'm not going with you. Go to your condo," she said dryly. It took everything in me not to slap the shit out of her.

"Nic. I'm gon' ask one more fucking time. Get up and get yo ass in the fucking car! We leaving," I said, and walked out.

She must've saw I meant business, cause she did as she was told. On the way home, she didn't say a word, and I did not give a fuck at all.

We got home, and I put KJ in his playpen. I walked into our room and she tried to rush past me. I grabbed her jaw, squeezed the fuck out of it, and threw her back on the bed with force.

"Ow!" she yelped in pain.

"Don't you ever leave like that again!" I yelled.

"Or what?!" she yelled.

"Or I'm leaving this relationship!" I blurted out, and immediately regretted it.

"Oh, so I go spend the night at my mother's, and you threaten to leave me. But you went and fucked another bitch and I stayed. Cool."

"Nic, you know I didn't mean that. I'm sorry I-"

"Save it, Kendrick," she cut me off and went to shower.

I waited a minute, then entered the bathroom. I got in the shower with her and watched her let the water run over her sexy body. It wet her long hair, causing it to curl. She looked at me, then turned her back to me and let the water hit the front of her body. I saw her jaw was bruised from me squeezing it. I came behind her and hugged her tight, letting my dick hit her plump ass. I expected her to resist, but she didn't. I kissed her bruised jaw, and she tensed up and closed her eyes from the pain.

"I didn't mean to hurt your jaw," I said between the kisses I planted on her jaw line.

"First Michael, now you," she said as tears strolled her face.

I felt like shit. This nigga just whooped her ass, and here I was putting my hands on her too. "I'm sorry, babe," was all I could say.

"You been having to say that too much," she cried.

"I know. I'm gonna do better, I promise."

She didn't respond. I turned her to face me so I could inspect her jaw, and she avoided eye contact. "Nic, I love you so much you don't understand. You and Kendrick mean the world to me. If I hurt you, it's not intentional." I kissed her neck, then kneeled down and began to kiss from her stomach to her pussy, while holding her waist. I lifted one of her legs and began to lick and suck on her clit. I lifted her leg higher for more access, and dipped my tongue in her opening.

"Kendrick...uhhghhhh," she came, and I lapped it all up.

I picked her up and brought her tight pussy onto my long, thick dick. I pounded into her, and all you heard was our moans and the smacking of our wet skin as I tore that shit up. I bit my lip and looked her in the eyes as I went to work. Her pretty face made my dick harder, and she came on cue. I sucked and bit her lips as I slowed down my strokes.

"MMM," was all I could say. I could live in this pussy.

She wrapped her arms around me, bringing her body closer as I held her up, and placed soft kisses on my biceps, making me want to nut early as fuck. She started kissing and sucking my neck, making me moan like a little hoe. The neck kisses, plus the feeling of her wet tight walls was too much; a nigga felt high. Eyes closed and shit. Scrunching my face and everything.

"Ahh!" I moaned, sounding like a bitch almost.

"Daddy!! I'm about to cum again!!!" she moaned.

I tongued her down as she came hard on my dick. I sped up, she leaned back, and I devoured her nipples on her firm, round titties and played with her nipple rings. I released into her, and we continued to kiss. I let her down off my dick.

"I love your crazy ass, Kendrick," she said, licking my chin and sucking my bottom lip.

"I love you too," I said, grabbing her neck, biting my lip, and tonguing her down.

She dropped to her knees, rubbed my head on her soft lips, then deep throated me until my toes curled and I busted in her mouth. She swallowed it all with her lil freaky ass. I had never moaned in that high of an octave in my life as I did with her. I loved that niggas didn't know how freaky she was. I literally was able to put it anywhere except her eyes, nose, and ears. Nic was an A1 pornstar in the bedroom; my wish was her command. My bitch knew how to please her nigga, contrary to popular belief. We washed each other and she made us breakfast. As crazy as she made me, I loved this woman.

Chapter Five: Jessica Leon

When Christy told me she had gotten married in Vegas to Kayden, it made me sad as hell. I was happy for her, but I felt like Kendon and I were getting nowhere. I had a feeling he was messing around, because it was in my gut. Kendon was a hoe by nature, and no matter how he tried to pretend like he changed, I knew how he was. I just did what most girls do; hoped he would change for me.

They recently hired this new girl named Honey, and after they hired her ass, Kendon seemed to frequent KB's way more as a customer than an owner. I decided to drop the fuck by. I didn't tell my friends, because I know they would say, "if you look you will find." Well, that was too damn bad. I would die before I let this nigga fuck around on me.

I pulled into the back parking lot and I saw his car. Hoe ass nigga. It was a Friday around 8pm, and the place was jumping. I walked in and said hi to the doorman, who knew me.

"Where is Kendon?" I asked.

He pointed to a group of niggas who I realized we're Jules, Maurice, Ricky, and dumb ass Kendon. The DJ announced Honey, and them niggas sat up like groupies at a concert. It pissed me off. She walked out and she was beautiful. Her skin was golden brown; she had long golden blond curls, honey colored eyes, and was stacked. She reminded me of Beyoncé. Ironically,

"Partition" by Beyoncé was playing. All the niggas in the club stood up to watch this hoe. I kept my eyes on Kendon, and I'd never seen him smile so hard. She grabbed the pole and seductively slid down, it causing the dollar bills to start flying. Kendon was definitely throwing money like he had never seen pussy in his life. She turned her back to us and touched her toes, giving us full view of her plump round ass. You would've thought this was a Michael Jackson concert the way these niggas was getting ready to faint. She climbed up the pole, twirled down, and mami landed in a split. By this point, even I was amazed. The floor of the stage was covered in so many bills that you couldn't see it anymore. She finished her dance, and then the DJ brought her the mic.

"Now I need a special guest up here tonight," she said, causing all the thirsty niggas to howl and shit. I was so happy Kendon kept quiet. "One that can keep his hands to himself. Hmmm," she said as she looked around the packed room. "Well, we have an actual King brother here tonight, so might as well. Come on, Kendon!" she yelled laughing, and everybody cheered him on. I felt like I was gon' throw up.

They turned on "Body Party" by Ciara, and she went to work on Kendon, grinding on him and all kinds of shit. I felt tears welling up, and I got hot all over. When she was done, she leaned down and whispered something in his ear, causing him to smack and grab her ass. She giggled, and the crowd cheered his corny ass on. She said her goodbye to the crowd and went backstage as Kendon came back down to sit with his friends. I left without him knowing I was there, and sped to his home. I was going to simply go to my house and never talk to him again, but I wanted to confront his ass first.

***

I waited and waited for him until I saw it was 4am. I logged into his iCloud and went to Find My iPhone. I located his shit and wrote down the address he was at. I drove there in what I had on, a spaghetti-strapped top and yoga shorts, and then I threw on tennis shoes. My hair was in a bun, and I made sure I put Vaseline on my face. I was fighting tonight!

I pulled up to the address and parked. I said a prayer that I didn't kill this nigga, then hopped out. "Ayo" by Chris Brown and Tyga was bumping loud as hell, and I heard a lot of voices. I walked in the door, which was wide open, and searched and looked around the party. I saw Honey and Kendon dancing together outside in the backyard where everyone mostly was. I felt so weak and broken; I felt like I couldn't even fight. I walked up and tapped him on the shoulder. The bystanders knew some shit was about to pop, because I wasn't in party attire. Kendon turned around and bucked his eyes. I punched his ass in the nose, and he fell back.

"Who the fuck are you?!" Honey yelled like this was her nigga I punched.

I didn't even talk. I kicked that bitch in her stomach, causing her to trip over the ice chest. I lunged on top of her and started fucking her up. I ripped so many tracks out her head, I doubt she had any left. She reached up for my bun and I bit the shit out of her forearm, causing her to scream. I felt Kendon grab me, so elbowed him in the nuts.

"Get this bitch off me!" she yelled as I banged her head into the cement.

Her face was bloody as fuck, and I was satisfied. I got off her and kicked her ass so fucking hard in the neck, making her cough. I took the ice chest and dumped all the water, ice, and bottled drinks on Kendon, causing him to scream.

"You bitch ass nigga!" I yelled before storming out. The people at the party were quiet as hell, and the music was off by the time I was done.

"Jess...Je…Jessica!" I heard Kendon yell after me.

"Fuck off hoe!" I yelled over my shoulder.

I sped to the home we shared and locked myself in the guest room. I cried hard until I drifted off to sleep.

***

"Wake your crazy ass up!" I heard Kendon yell.

I opened my eyes to see him standing over me looking like someone whooped his ass, which made me happy. The part from Friday when Chris Tucker said, "You got knocked the fuck out!" popped in my head.

"Don't trip. I'm out," I said, sitting up. My body was sore from kicking so much ass.

"You out?!" he laughed like a psycho.

"Yeah nigga. I'm not fucking with you no more. We a wrap!" I got out the bed, and he slapped the shit out of me. "I told yo ass not to touch me or I was gon' fuck you up!" he yelled.

I hopped up and starting wailing on this nigga. He grabbed my hair, threw me into the dresser, and it knocked the wind out of me. He charged me, and backhanded me to the floor.

"Get yo ass up! You want to fight like a nigga, let's go!"

I tried to crawl away, and he kicked me in the back, and I collapsed. "Kendon! Stop!!" I screamed through tears.

He grabbed my face and banged it on the floor, "Shut up with that fucking crying! You a nigga, so act like one!"

I stood up finally, and he slapped me again, busting my lip. I grabbed my hurting face and continued to cry. "Yeah, cry like the little bitch you are! You ain't no damn dude, so stop acting like you one!" he said, then pushed me into the wall and left.

I couldn't wrap my mind around what happened. My whole body ached. I slid down the wall and continued to cry until I couldn't anymore.

***

I laid on the floor the whole day. I watched the sun come up and go down. Kendon hadn't returned once. I looked at the clock and it was 12am. I looked in the mirror and my face was messed up. I started crying again just as Kendon burst through, the door causing me to jump.

"No Kendon. Don't!" I pleaded with my hands up.

"Ain't nobody gon' hit yo ass! Shut the fuck up!" he spat.

"Just ju…just let me get my stuff and I will go home," I said with a shaken voice.

He closed the door. "Before you do that, I want to know why you came to that party and acted crazy," he said, folding his arms.

Tears were flowing freely out of my swollen eyes. "I uhm…you and Honey. I saw you with her," I said, almost in a whisper.

"Saw me doing what?! I did nothing with her," he frowned.

"I saw her dancing on you and giving you a lap dance," I said.

He laughed loud as hell. "So because you saw us dancing. You showed up at someone's house and beat them up. And then me too."

"Kendon. What I saw was not innocent. I know you. You've fucked her before," I said slowly.

"So now what?" he asked.

"So, now. You ...and I are done," I said through sniffles. I was crying like a baby.

"Why Jessica? Because you think I slept with another girl?"

"Because you did. And then you came in here hitting me!" I yelled.

"Jessica. I'm sorry, but I told you to stop putting your hands on me, and you kept doing that shit. Kept pushing me, punching me, you just as bad. I'm supposed to just let you break my nose and black my fucking eye when you feel like?" he asked.

"Kendon, I'm sorry but I love you and you don't understand how it feels to see you cheat on me!"

"Jessica. I did not sleep with that hoe! She is interested in Kendrick, anyway. But even if she wasn't, I wouldn't cheat on you. I made you a promise! I was just having a good time. And just cause you see me doing stuff that makes you unhappy, you can't go hitting on me like that!" he spat.

I plopped down on the bed and started crying. He was right. Yes, it was wrong for him to hit on me, but I was no better. Every time he upset me, no matter how big or small, I would black his eye, break his nose, crush his rib, slap him, anything.

"Baby don't cry, you know I love you. And I know you're not this monster that you go on acting like. I didn't want to hit you. I'm sorry, but I was tired of you hitting on me and then acting like we was cool after. But again, I'm sorry," he said, sitting next to me. He lifted my face out my hands and kissed all over my messed up face.

"You still love me? I still love your crazy ass," he smiled.

I smiled, although painful, and shook my head yes. He ran me a hot bubble bath in the big Jacuzzi tub, picked me up, and took me to the bathroom to put me in it. He cleaned my whole body, and even washed my hair. He toweled me off and laid me in the bed. He cuddled up to me, face to face, and kissed me softly on my messed up lip.

"I love you, Jessica. We can make this work if you just trust me and start treating me like your man, and not something you own," he said softly.

I nodded in agreement. "Can I still curse a bitch out if she too friendly?" I half joked.

"Of course ma, that's your job." I turned my back to him, and he cuddled up behind me and kissed the nape of my neck and shoulders. We fell asleep just like that.

Chapter Six: Danielle Moore

It was the night of Christy's 19th birthday, and she was having a party at one of the hottest clubs in Baltimore. I'm not surprised she was able to get a 21 and over club to let her host her birthday there. She was married to Kayden, who just got a record contract, and she was associated with the biggest kingpins in the city. Tia and I were happy to get an invite, because we still hadn't bagged a boss. I planned to get one and run off with his ass; I wasn't going to 12th grade.

We walked in the club and it was turnt. The bar was fully stocked, and all the hits were blasting. Currently they were playing "Commas" by Future. I got up to the VIP area and the 4 stooges–Nic, Morgan, Jessica, and Christy–were dancing in a circle with each other, singing the song. Their men were chilling, smiling at them. I rolled my eyes. The club waitress brought a cake out for Christy, and Kayden took the mic, making the club go crazy.

"I just want to say Happy Birthday to the best wife a nigga can have. I love you Christy, and I can't wait to celebrate many more birthdays with you, girl," he said, smiling and the crowd cheered.

Tia and I rolled our eyes. He reached in his pocket and pulled out a remote key.

"It's to a Porsche!!" Christy screamed into the mic.

The club cheered, and Nic, Morgan, and Jessica's faces lit up. Kayden kissed her lips and handed the mic to Nic.

"Christy! I love you. I love how you've always had my back no matter what! Happy birthday honey," Nic said as she handed Christy a velvet box with a bracelet.

"Crazy Christy! You know how I feel about you, and I'm so happy your life has come full circle and so early! I love you baby. Happy birthday!" Morgan said, and walked her pregnant self to add a charm to the bracelet.

"Be careful with my baby, girl!" Kendreeis joked. Christy was now crying.

Jessica grabbed the mic, and she and Christy cheesed at each other. "Mami!!!! You know you been my bitch forever! There are no words to explain my love for you, chica. Happy birthday! I love you!" Jessica walked another charm over to add to the bracelet.

"We all have the same one now, and each charm means something special. We will always be connected, no matter what," Nic told her.

The club cheered, and the DJ told Christy happy birthday before cutting back on the music.

The VIP bouncer walked to Kendrick "Hey, it's a young man wanting to talk to you."

"What's his name?"

"French, he said." The bouncer shrugged. Kendrick and his brothers laughed so hard.

"Let this nigga through, but let Draco check him first," Kendon said.

They guy they called French strutted in, and he was fine as hell. He was caramel-skinned, bald, and had a perfectly lined goatee. He was dressed in a black button-up that was unbuttoned at the top showing his chiseled chest, jeans, a velvet material blazer, with Gucci loafers.

"Bingo Danielle!" Tia said, reading my mind.

Kendrick rubbed his short beard and his short curly fro that he decided to keep, with his sexy ass. He had a scruffy look to him now. French sat across from the fine ass brothers and smiled hard as hell. They chatted for a bit, and then he shook their hands and left. He walked by, and I cut him off.

"Danielle." I said.

He looked me up and down in my short ass dress and stilettos. I had Senegalese twists in as well.

"Danielle, I like you. But before we move forward, who is that?" he whispered, pointing to Nic. *Here we fucking go*, I thought.

"My cousin. But she is taken. She is Kendrick's girl," I whispered back, attempting to waver him off her. He looked at Kendrick and bounced his head up as if to say what's up.

"And her?" he asked, pointing to Christy.

"Her best friend, and Kayden's wife," I replied.

"Uh hunh. Ooh damn, and Cassie over there?" he asked, irritating the fuck out of me.

"Morgan, but she is pregnant as you can see, and dating Kendreeis," I replied and he nodded.

"What about the firecracker right there?" he asked, referring to Jessica.

"Jessica, she is Kendon's," I started, being short; this nigga was pissing me off.

"All bad as fuck. M!" He turned back to me. "And who you belong to?" he asked.

"You," I replied. He smiled and looked at Tia, who waved seductively.

"Get your friend and let's go," he said.

Tia and I hurried out the VIP and out the club to follow him.

***

We arrived to his hotel, and he told Tia and I to strip. We did. "Now kiss," he said.

He watched us tongue it up, as he stroked his twelve-inch dick. I was scared as hell, but before Gina left, she and Paris used to tell us that this was a part of getting a baller. I was gon' do whatever French wanted.

"Touch each other," he instructed.

Tia began to suck my nipple while playing with my clit. "Ahhhahhuuhhhh," I moaned. That shit felt good. I soon came all over her fingers, which she licked. I pushed her back and kissed from her stomach to her pussy. I started licking and sucking her clit, while fingering her. She was moaning loud as hell. She came all over my mouth, and she tasted good.

French was hard as a rock watching us, and instructed me to suck his huge dick. I could barely fit it in my mouth. Tia was sucking on his balls, but because I couldn't fit him fully in my mouth, he instructed her to take care of the base of his dick.

"Damn, fuck!!" he moaned as he fucked my face. He pulled out and came all over both of our faces.

"Turn around," he ordered. We did as we were told, and he took turns fucking us doggy style. He would switch back and forth.

"Take this dick, young bitch!" he yelled as he rammed into me and pulled my hair. I came on his dick, and he smacked my ass. He entered Tia from behind and tore the lining out her shit.

"Ahhhh French…Ah!" she begged him to slow down, but he didn't.

I was starting to think she was a virgin. She dried up, and he slapped the shit out of her, knocking her off the bed. He pulled me back to him and rammed into me until he came all over my ass.

"Nothing like young pussy!" he said, out of breath. "Go clean y'all selves up!" he spat.

We had nut all on our faces, ass, and breast. When we came back out, he tongued us down.

"Now, I want y'all to lure your four little friends from the club, here one by one. Once I make them my bitches too, I'll be satisfied, he said. "In the meantime, you need to hang with your cousin more. Get me all the info you can on her nigga's operation so I can snatch the rug from under them niggas!" he said to me.

He laughed, then pulled out some coke. "Come try some for daddy." We did as we were told.

Chapter Six: Kayden King

All was good on the home front with Christy and me. I had just signed a record contract, so business was good too. The only thing was the street business. This nigga French, that came to talk at Christy's birthday, had to be the dumbest nigga alive. The way he did that nigga Houston was known by every kingpin and hustler in America damn near. The fact that he tried to talk about merging with us was laughable, and that's what we did; laughed at that nigga.

I told Christy to watch her mouth around Nic's cousin, because I saw her fast ass leave with him. I knew he was a snake, and he'd try to use her dumb ass to his advantage. What other reason would a 35-year-old nigga be interested in some 17-year-old girls? I don't fucking know. Unless he just a pedophile, which I'm sure he was as well as a professional snake. He requested to meet with my cousins and I about merging. I don't even know why we was entertaining him. I think it was funny to hear what this dumb nigga had to say. We decided to meet today, because we were all flying to California so Kendrick and Nic could get married finally.

I arrived at one of the dummy condos that Kendrick had. He frequented it enough to make it look as if he really stayed there. The place was about 40 miles from his actual home he shared with Nic. We all had at least two condos/really nice apartments that were a minimum of 30 miles away from the real deal. We made sure the condos were decked the fuck out, because who would believe some rich niggas like us are living in dirty ass complexes or condo? It was the same with our cars. We always parked our "dummy" cars at these places, and then our real and expensive cars at our actual homes. Dummy cars were parked in our garages around back at our real homes. That way if a nigga drove by our real home by happenstance, he wouldn't recognize the car. We only used the "real" vehicles to drive to far places for dates, vacations, and shit. They all had dark ass tint so when we were local, no one would know who was driving it. Anything local, we used our fake whips. Confusing I know, but this shit been working for years and was taught to us by my uncle Kairio and father Kylin; all to protect where we laid our heads.

My brother Khayman was against this protocol, cause he said it was no need, but he ended up dead pretty much because of it. He was too reckless and never checked to make sure he wasn't being followed. After a big transaction one day, he went home to relax. Some people that had been gunning for us at the time ran up in his crib, robbed him, and emptied 4 shots between his eyes. At that time, my cousins and I were just working the trap houses for my dad and uncle, and they were still running things. That was the second loss my father and I had in less than a year. My mother had a rare heart disease that weakened her immune system. One day she caught a cold and it killed her. My father Kylin is super protective of me and my cousins, cause I think he feels he can’t take another loss.

My cousins and I were all different, but we worked well together like a puzzle. Kendrick was the logical one, and if we needed a plan or system, he always could come up with something. That was why my father and uncle chose him to run the shit. Kendreeis was a hot head and didn't think twice before beating a nigga's ass or killing someone. He could be reckless at times too, which is why my dad and uncle skipped over him to hold the reigns. Kendon was just laid back and was more so the listener. You give him the run down and he could carry it out to the tee. He wasn't reckless, but he'd kill your ass too. He was that quiet person in class that surprised you when he beat the bully's ass. My brother Khayman was just an irrational thug. I loved that nigga, but he was crazy as hell and never planned shit. He and Kendreeis were a lot alike, except Kendreeis is a little more logical and thinks ahead more. Last but not least, there is ya boy. I'm more like Kendon, where I just prefer to carry out the plans. However, I tend to stray and do my own shit if I feel it is necessary. I'm a bit more outspoken than Kendon. All in all, I love my niggas and the loyalty we have to one another is out of this world.

***

We were all sitting in Kendrick's plush ass office, when Draco escorted French into the room.

"What's up y'all! Kendrick? This shit is nice, man. Where's your wifey?" he came in, smiling.

"Thank you. And why?"

"Oh, just wanted to say hi," he smiled, looking goofy as hell.

"No need for that. Sit down," Kendrick ordered and pointed to a chair.

Kendreeis was high as hell, and smirking at the nigga. I couldn't look at him, cause I knew we'd burst into laughter at this corny ass old nigga.

"So speak," Kendon said.

"Well, as y'all may or may not know, I'm the king of the city in Chicago and I wanted to see about merging our shit and pretty much expanding us," he grinned, showing a couple dingy gold teeth. I almost threw up.

"I heard you in the business of pimping too," I spoke up.

"Well yeah. I make sure I have multiple incomes! Know what I'm saying!" he started laughing and clapping his hands. Everyone else was silent, so he cleared his throat out of obvious embarrassment. "So what y'all say, King men?" he asked with his hands out.

Kendrick looked in the air, "I say. Do you think I'm a fool?" He then locked eyes with French.

"A fool! Well nah! Why you say that?" he chuckled nervously, while looking around at all of us.

"Well, I know how you became the king of Chicago. Let's just say that," Kendrick spat.

"Well that was a long time ago. I'm sincere here," he pleaded.

"Okay nigga. Your time is up. I don't want to see you sniffing around here no more. You take your bum ass back to Chicago, or go try this bullshit on another nigga, but it ain't happening over here! I don't get down with snake niggas like you. You pissing me off by even thinking that I'd be dumb enough to get up with you. Get the fuck up and get yo weak ass out my face, nigga! And if I ever hear you asking about my wife again, I'm gon' put your egg head ass through a meat grinder," Kendrick spat.

French got up like he wanted war, making us all stand up. He obviously weighed his options in his head, then stormed out. Kendreeis finally busted up laughing, and Kendrick tried to stay frowning but he couldn't help it.

"We need to find some new trap houses, cause I know his ass knows where a couple of the current ones are. While we looking, we need to have each house pretty much as empty as possible without our niggas running out of product. Gon' be hard, but it's the only way. We need to figure out the average amount we sell a day from each house and only supply that to each house. If the nigga happens to need more, we will provide it. Make note of the house and man that requested more, prior to giving it to him. That way, if it's a set up, we know exactly who the fuck it was. No need for a game of clue. I will let Damien and Ricky know, because they collect and do first count. We been robbed twice already fucking with Jermaine's disloyal ass, and then Houston's bitch ass. If we take another hit, uncle and pops gon' try to take back over. We been soft, I feel like. We need to be out here watching non-stop, and killing any nigga that even breathe like he a snake. However they breathe. Y’all got it?!" Kendrick said.

"Hell yeah!" we said in unison.

"I know y'all told me to fall back a bit, but I can't. Not until this shit is running smoothly again," I said. They all nodded in agreement, and I was happy they did.

Chapter Six: Jimmy French

Them Similac breath niggas had me fucked up. I was old enough to be all they daddy, and for them to think could just dismiss me like that was actually laughable. You damn right I planned to snake through that operation and take over like I did in the Chi. I planned to get all they bitches and put them on my stroll, too. I could make so much money with they little fine asses working for me. Young pussy always made the most money.

I left Chicago cause my shit had fell apart; it was a mess. My traps constantly got robbed, and I had too many snake niggas around me. I wanted the King Brothers shit because they ran their shit with structure. I let Houston mentor me before I took over, and I've learned he didn't know what the fuck he was doing. He ran his shit with all talk and no action, and I did the same. I threatened to kill nigga's all the time, but I never did. Long story short, niggas got hip to that and start rebelling and turning on a nigga. You can pretty much say I have no operation back home. I wasn't good at being a drug boss, but I was a natural at pimping. Why didn't I stick to one? I felt you got more respect when you ran a drug operation. Only people that respected pimps were women, but everybody respected a kingpin. I wanted to learn the King Brothers strategy like the back of my hand, then pull the rug from under they wet behind the ear asses. I was happy I had Danielle, because she was a direct shoe in. I would tell her what to try to pry from Nic, and I'd be ready. Since them niggas wouldn't accept me, I needed Danielle to do more than originally planned.

***

I pulled up to my hotel room and gave my keys to valet. I walked into my room and saw Tia and Danielle sleep in the bed, still naked from me wearing them out this morning.

"Wake up!" I yelled loud as hell, and they jumped. "Y'all ready to start making me some money?" I asked, taking my blazer off.

"This early, I -" Tia attempted to speak up, but was stuttering like a little bitch.

"I'm sorry, that was a rhetorical question; y'all starting tonight. Now come suck daddy's dick. I want to make sure you pleasing the clientele!" I instructed her.

"Come on Danielle!" Tia said, grabbing her arm.

"No, I said you, not Danielle," I yelled. She got on my damn nerves.

She got up and walked over to me slow as fuck. Her perky titties made my dick hard. I unleashed my twelve inches and she dropped to her knees. She started teasing the tip, and then put half in her mouth.

"All of it!" I yelled.

"I can't!" she yelped. I slapped her ass so hard that her nose was bleeding.

"Ah!" she screamed, holding her face.

I slapped her with my dick to remind her of what I asked her to do. She started sucking my dick and finally she made it disappear. After a couple times up and down my shaft, and once it was getting good, she vomited all over my dick. I punched her ass so hard it hurt my hand. Danielle got up and wiped me off. Once she was done, I continued to whoop Tia's ass. She stood up, and I slapped her across the room, making her fall on the lamp and break it. I grabbed her by the hair, and held her face back so I could punch it multiple times. After about ten hard punches, she started to drift in and out of consciousness. I let go of her hair and she dropped to the ground. I kicked her in the stomach one last time hard as hell, causing her to scream. I stormed to the door and yelled for them to be ready when I returned later that night. Dumb bitches.

Chapter Six: Kendreeis King

After that waste of a fucking time ass meeting, I called Morgan and told her I was taking her to dinner. Her being pregnant, she didn't really go anywhere. Also, she decided to take online classes for college this year so I knew that made her sad.

When I arrived, she was sitting on the couch dressed, looking beautiful. She had on a tan dress that was snug to her small body, but showed her stomach of course. She had on tan stilettos, which I didn't approve of, but I wasn't gon' ruin her night by being daddy daycare. Her hair was in a low ponytail with a part down the middle. She had on nude lipstick and gold-flaked eye shadow.

"Close your mouth, Diddy," she joked as she walked over to me.

That nigga Diddy could not close his mouth, even when resting. Ironically, she was identical to Cassie. I chuckled at her little diss.

"You look beautiful, Morgan. I'm just in awe. Damn, can't a nigga as fly as me be in awe of someone other than myself for a change?!" I joked, making us both chuckle.

I was already dressed cause of that meeting, so I opened the front door back up.

***

We arrived at this steakhouse about 10 minutes from the house. I got out and opened the door for her, and put out my hand to assist her.

"Thank you babe," she said, and kissed my lips.

"I hate that sticky shit!" I frowned and wiped my mouth.

"But you love me."

"I do," I smirked, and rubbed her huge stomach.

We walked into the restaurant, hand in hand, and I gave the host my name for our reservation. "I've never been to a place this fancy," Morgan beamed.

"I know, that's why I brought you here. My dad used to bring my mom here a lot. He always said, *only take the special ones here, or if you super hard up for pussy*, but that should never be the case," I told her, and we both laughed.

The waiter walked over and took our drink orders. I knew Morgan ass was gon' get iced tea.

"I'm so hungry!" she said, looking over the menu.

"Trust me, I know."

"So you saying I'm fat?"

"Not at all. You was too small to begin with."

"Good answer nigga!" she spat, and we both laughed. We enjoyed each other's company and ate these huge ass pasta dishes. She finished hers, and I had to get a to-go box. *Damn. Lol.*

"Before we go Morgan, I want to talk to you."

"Uh oh," she bucked her eyes.

"I love you, like a lot," I chuckled nervously. I still couldn't believe I was telling a girl that I loved her. I used to live by the motto *bitches ain't shit but hoes and tricks*. "And you've changed me. I used to be angry and just always about killing and trapping. I never saw myself being somebody's boyfriend, or husband, or nothing, until I met you. My mother always told me when I met the right girl, I would know, but I never believed it." I continued. Morgan was tearing up, and it made me laugh.

"I'm so lucky to have met you Morgan, and I know it's hard dealing with me sometimes, especially when I get all angry and irrational, but I appreciate you. I'm so happy we have a baby coming," I said, and stood up. I walked over to her and kneeled down. "Morgan, I don't see any reason why we shouldn't make this more official. I love you more than anything, and I plan to be with you forever. I promise I will make you happy and be the best father to our baby or babies. Will you do me the honor of being my wife?" She was crying so hard that her mascara was running. I chuckled at her.

"Of course, Kendreeis!" she said through tears as I slid the 14-carat diamond ring onto her finger. The whole restaurant cheered, reminding me we were in public. I smiled and planted a kiss on her lips. "Morgan King. Has a ring to it," she said as we started to eat dessert.

"Yeah it does," I smiled.

I breathed a sigh a relief once it was done. I was 99.9% sure she'd say yes, but I was still scared as hell. I needed it to be perfect, and it was; just like her.

Chapter Six: Tia Alexander

Danielle and I were dressed and ready to head out the door for our first day of work. Look at me, making it sound like we work in retail. This shit was scary as hell. French gave us strict orders about how things worked and how much to charge. We were to do any and everything these niggas wanted, no matter what it was.

Danielle had on a tight black dress and simple, sexy, black stilettos. She had her hair up in a big bun on top of her head, and her baby hairs were laid. I had my hair down in its curly state, and a tight red dress. My shoes were red also, and my make up was flawless. Danielle didn't need to wear make up, because her pretty mocha skin had a natural glow to it, plus she had a mole like Marilyn Monroe right above her full lips. I always wondered why Danielle couldn't get a King brother, because she was literally the prettiest girl I had ever seen. Way prettier than Nic, or any of her friends.

"You okay?" Danielle asked, snapping me out of my thoughts.

"Yeah I'm okay, just a little scared. You?" I asked, looking over at her as we finally walked passed a McDonalds and arrived at our spot.

"Yeah I'm okay," she replied.

"Who is that staring at you?" I asked her, noticing some young guy staring. He was super cute, and looked like he had his shit together. He was talking to some guy, but staring a hole through Danielle. Once he finished his conversation, he hopped in his Lexus truck and sped off.

"No idea, but clearly he didn't want what we had to offer," she said, making us both laugh.

A black truck pulled up to us, and the passenger window rolled down. Some big buff nigga flashed a mouth full of gold, and it made me frown slightly. All I thought about was French's old penny breath ass. Once I realized I was frowning, I tried to turn it into a smile. I'm sure it was the worst smile ever; try frowning and making it into a smile. Not cute.

"Come closer ladies, I don't bite," he said. *Please don't, I might get an infection*, I thought. Danielle and I walked over to his window, and waited for him to speak. "Get in," he said. Danielle's sneaky ass hopped in the backseat, making me have to get in the front and sit next to him. I rolled my eyes at her and she smiled.

"What you trying to get into?" I asked him, hoping we could get this over with.

"I got a room, I want to take y'all back to and chill. How much for simple intercourse with both of y'all," he asked, driving to what I assumed was his hotel.

"$1100 each!" Danielle lied. I snapped my neck to her and frowned.

"Aight $2200. That's cool." he replied, surprising the fuck out of me. I looked back at Danielle, and she cocked her head to the left and smiled. I laughed.

We arrived at his hotel. It was nice as hell and decked the fuck out. He had to be wack in the bedroom, cause there was no reason a nigga with all this money should have to pay for sex. He wasn't bad looking either, with clothes on. He was tall and stalky, with a low curly fro and gold teeth. He definitely didn't have a six-pack or anything, but he didn't appear to be fat as fuck either.

"Make yourself comfortable, ladies," he said, opening a bottle of champagne. This nigga was trying to have a date night and shit. The more he prolonged the sex, the better anyway.

"Thank you," Danielle and I said in unison as he handed us the champagne glasses.

After drinking a couple glasses of some bomb ass champagne that had to cost a couple racks, we started to smoke a couple blunts. He then turned on "Songs on 12 Play" by Chris Brown and Trey Songz. He walked over and started to kiss my neck, and I wasn't turned on at all. He was slobbering all over my neck, and it made me turn my lip up in disgust. He then switched over to Danielle, thank God. I wiped my neck off with the comforter. After drenching Danielle in his nasty drool, he asked us to take off our clothes and we did. He ran his ashy fingers over our bodies, admiring what he saw. All this money and the nigga had ashy fingers.

"Rub on it," he told me.

I did as he asked, even though I didn't want to, cause he was just so wack. His dick was definitely nothing to brag about. I could see why he had to pay for sex, because no bitch would willingly sit on that otherwise. I started to move my hand up and down on his dick, and he started to jerk a little.

"Ah fuck!" he moaned, and I turned my head in order not to look at him. "Let your girl sit on it," he said, reaching over and slapping my ass. I thanked God, and removed my hand from his dick before he could even finish his request.

"You need to strap up," Danielle told him, sliding her panties on and grabbing her dress.

"Come on ma. Chill," he said grinning, looking and back and forth between Danielle and I.

"Nah, you need to put a condom on first," Danielle said, folding her arms fully clothed again.

"Get yo ass over here, bitch! Y'all fuck niggas raw all the time, I'm sure!" he yelled loud as hell. I started to get scared, so I grabbed my underwear when he wasn't looking and slid them on slowly. I reached for my dress and brought it over my head as well.

"No we don't actually," Danielle spat back, standing her ground. French told us we needed to do whatever, but that was Danielle, always doing whatever the fuck she wanted. He stood up and Danielle grabbed my wrist as we booked it out the room.

"I already paid you stupid bitches!" I heard him yell after us.

I looked over my shoulder and saw him running out his room, trying to slide on his jeans at the same time. His stomach was jiggling, and so were his breasts. This nigga needed to hit the gym ASAP! We kept running and hurried onto the elevator, where we pressed the 'door close' button until it finally closed. We ran outside the hotel and waved a taxi down. Once in the taxi, Danielle and I looked at each other and started dying laughing. We made $2200 and did absolutely nothing. We both stopped laughing after awhile, and silence fell upon us as we realized we still had to be out there and work. We still had to go home to French tonight. I was screaming on the inside.

Chapter Six: Nic Fuller

I was doing one of my last assignments for my class. In one week, I would be in sunny California getting married to my love, and I couldn't wait. I smiled, thinking about it as I typed. I heard the door and I got up to see him. Kendrick walked in wearing a hoodie, jeans, and sneakers. He had on the small gold chain with the "N" and a watch to match. I loved his little curly fro he decided to keep.

"Hey babe," he said as he leaned his head back on the door.

"What's wrong?" I asked, walking to him and hugging him tight, inhaling his cologne. "I made you salmon," I told him and kissed his lips.

"I need to talk to you," he said, grabbing my hand and walking me back into the den area.

My stomach dropped, cause the last time he said that, he told me he cheated. If he did that shit again, this was a wrap. As much as I loved him, I wouldn't allow him to be unfaithful throughout our relationship. We sat down on the couch, and he took both my hands in his. This was all too familiar, and my heartbeat sped up.

"I love you Nic. And I can't wait to marry you, but we gon' have to push it back," he sighed.

I was relieved that he hadn't cheated, but upset at pushing my wedding back. "Why?!"

"Because we got somebody on our backs right now, and we need to take care of some business. Right now this shit is too shaky to leave and be across the country," he pleaded.

"I can't do this, Kendrick," I said, standing up.

"Can't do what?!" he frowned, looking up at me.

"This bullshit! You proposed months and months ago, and there is always a new fucking reason why we can't get married just yet!" I yelled.

"Lower your damn voice when you speak to me first off, and secondly, shit happens! I'm not making this shit up!"

"Well, Kendrick when you are ready to be a family, you let me know," I said, turning to walk away.

"Nic, baby. I promise as soon as this shit is taken care of, I will marry you baby. Please understand me," he pleaded with my hand in his.

"That's the problem! This relationship is all about Kendrick, and what Kendrick needs, or wants. This shit ain't never about me, unless it benefits you. I move in when you want. I have a baby when you want. We only go out when you want. And now we get married when you want," I shook my head.

"Well damn. You sound unhappy," he said, looking surprised.

"Of course I'm happy. I love you and love being with you. But sometimes I want things done on my time, or cause I want it or need it."

"Need it? You need me to marry you? Why?" he frowned.

"Because Kendrick!" I whined.

"I see. You think I'm gonna leave you and you don't want to be seen as just my baby mama," he chuckled.

"What's funny?" I frowned.

"Cause that's never gonna happen. You know how crazy I am about you, Nic. I almost bodied a nigga just cause he asked about you. I couldn't leave you if I wanted to. You got my heart, and I need you to know that. Forever," he said, lighting up his jade green eyes.

I smiled, "Well Kendrick, until you prove that, I can't be here. I'm going to go stay with my mom until you're ready to do what you need to do to keep me happy, like I've done for you. If you need to take care of business first to do so, then so be it. But I can't wait here for you. Just don't take too long."

I got up and packed me and KJ's stuff. I loved Kendrick, but I felt like he was stringing me along. If he didn't want to get married, he should say that, and I would be okay, but for him to pretend like it's just stuff in the way is cowardly, and that's not what I need right now. I need a man. Plus, if he really has shit to straighten out, me being gone should be a good thing, and he should be trying to get married soon. If not, I was gon' keep it pushing.

"Man, you fucking tripping!" he yelled as I brought a packed suitcase from upstairs.

"No, you tripping if you think I'm just gonna sit here and have your babies, just for you to come home one day and say you done with me!" I yelled through tears.

"I fucking love you, Nic! I would never do no shit like that! I'm stressed the fuck out trying to handle this shit and you giving me hell every damn time I come home is not helping! Damn!" he yelled, and threw a glass ashtray against the wall.

I jumped at the crash. "Then me being gone will help you."

"No it won't! All that's gonna do is stress me out, cause I won't know if you're safe or not! This nigga is the biggest snake of the century and I can't be worried about you being kidnapped and making sure my shit ain't getting robbed at the same time!" he yelled, then plopped down on the couch and ran his fingers over his face.

I hated how much I loved him sometimes. I walked over and sat next to him. I removed his face from his hands, and kissed all over his face. He grabbed my body close, and started tonguing me down.

"Kendrick, stop," I whispered. He continued to kiss me and leaned me back until he was on top of me in between my legs.

"Kendrick, I love you too much, and I need a stronger commitment from you," I said through tears.

"Baby, I'm gonna marry you I promise," he said in between kisses.

"When Kendrick?" I asked in a low tone.

"ASAP," he said, removing my clothes.

"Kendrick, I'm pregnant," I whispered.

I was on birth control so, I don't know how it happened, but then again, this nigga fucked me at least three times a day. Any time he saw me, he was getting inside me. I hadn't showered alone in months. I didn't complain though, cause I loved fucking my nigga, and holding out would send him to another bitch, which I was not having.

He smiled, bit his lip, and continued removing my clothes. He made love to me all night, right there on the couch. We fell asleep, and I woke up in the middle of the night. I quietly moved from under him, and grabbed KJ from his room. There was no way I could leave with Kendrick awake. I was too weak for him, and soon as he started laying on his charm, I would be unpacking my shit to stay. I needed him to know I was serious, especially being pregnant again.

Chapter Seven: Kendrick King

It had been a week and a half since Nic left and I was sick, but I had to take care of business. I tried to vent to my father, but he just pissed me off saying I needed to learn to balance my shit. I would learn to balance, but business had to come first right now. I tried calling her, texting, dropping by, asking her out, but got nothing. She was serious and refused to see me. I knew if I saw her, I'd be able to convince her to come home and she knew it too, which is why she refused. She didn't want to hear nothing I had to say, unless it was about the wedding. When it was time to see Kendrick Jr., she'd have her mother drop him off to me.

This nigga French was a snake ass perverted ass nigga, and I needed to make sure he was fucking gone. I tried to warn him to get out of town, but he didn't listen. I got word that this nigga's operation in Chicago was no more, and that was all the confirmation I needed to know he was after our shit. Two days after Nic snuck her pretty ass out of here, French had some niggas rob our trap house. Thank God the two niggas I had working it were able to overpower the bitchmade ass muthafuckas he sent. I made sure to have their heads delivered to his crib. Hopefully that was his dummy crib, but as dumb as this nigga was, it probably was actually where he lived now.

On top of that, he had Nic's little cousin Danielle and her friend Tia selling pussy. When I came to see Nic, she wouldn’t talk to me, and her mother made me promise to rescue Danielle. I wasn't captain save a hoe, but she was my baby girl's mom and I was gon' do it. Plus, I kind of felt bad for Danielle's dumb ass. On a lighter note, we had successfully switched out all our trap houses. We kept two of our old ones, just to throw the snakes in the grass off.

I was on the couch with my shirt off, getting high as fuck off some Kush. All I had on was my "N" chain and boxers. I was depressed without my baby girl, but I had to finish my shit. I heard keys in the door and I hopped up, waiting to see her. She walked in looking beautiful as ever. Her honey colored skin glistened, and her full lips made my mouth water. Her hair was up with some hanging down her sexy back. She had on yoga pants that showed off her small, round, plump ass that I loved to do all kinds of shit to. It looked a little fatter than usual, probably cause she was pregnant again. She had on a sports bra showing her piercings, and her stomach was toned and sexy, making me want to lick and bite and kiss it like I usually did.

"Nic, I uh…" I stuttered, looking like a strung out ass crack head.

"I'm just here to get some more clothes for KJ," she said, giving me a half smile.

"No hug or nothing? No love for your baby daddy?" I attempted to joke. She hesitated, then walked over to me, and I hugged her tight.

"Damn, baby girl. I missed you," I whispered. I began kissing her neck and collarbone, inhaling her sweet perfume. A nigga had been jacking off every night, and I missed her being in my arms when I went to sleep. I hadn't had to jack off in years.

"Kendrick…" she said in a low tone as I sucked and bit her lips. This is why she didn't want to see me. Ha.

I picked my head up and started tonguing her down. She wrapped her arms around my neck and melted in my embrace. I was rubbing my hands up and down her body. Putting my hands down the back of her pants, squeezing her ass, and feeling her pussy from the back. I fucking missed her so much.

"Come back, Nic. I need KJ and you here with me while you carrying my seed," I whispered in between kisses. She didn't respond, and I laid her on the couch and started removing her pants and panties together. She put her hands over mine to stop me.

"Just let me feel you babe, I been feining for you," I whispered, kissing her lips. She looked as if she was about to give in while I was kissing her, but snapped out of it.

“No Kendrick. You don't have those privileges anymore,” she lightly pushed me off.

“Oh yeah? You gave them to another nigga already, huh?” I blurted, like a dumb ass.

“You know what? I will buy him some more stuff. Bye Kendrick,” she hopped up and left.

“Nic! baby-” and like that she was gone.
“Fuck!!!” I yelled and plopped down on the couch.

I guess she let Kendreeis in, cause he walked into the den. "Ugh nigga! What the fuck?!" he yelled.

I looked down and saw my dick sticking straight up through the hole in my boxers; I was rock hard. Nic was def gon' give a nigga blue balls.

"Sorry man," I said as I grabbed the couch pillow and sat it in my lap.

"You good, nigga? You looking like a strung out Larenz Tate in Why Do Fools Fall In Love!" he said, laughing.

I laughed too. "Fuck you nigga! It's Nic. She got me losing it," I said in a low tone.

"I see. You need to get it together, Kendrick. How you gon' be a kingpin, and have a family, if you stressing already?" he asked.

"Whatever. Fuck Nic. We need to end this nigga French before he spits some more of his venom."

"Yeah nigga, I saw Tia on the streets and she looked miserable as hell. Maybe we can convince her to help us set that nigga up. Or get at his ass."

"Not Danielle?!" I asked.

"Nah, she too up that nigga's ass. She will tell him and give him a head start," he replied, and I nodded in agreement.

"Sounds like a plan. Who gon' go after her?" I asked.

"You. You know she got a thing for you," he smirked, and I shook my head. Women were causing me enough problems these days.

***

Three weeks had passed, and I finally saw Tia working. I drove on the side of her walking, and rolled down the window. Her face had a few bruises on it.

"Kendrick?!" she yelped in excitement. *Damn, shawty must be really feeling a nigga*, I thought.

"Yeah baby. Get in." Before I could finish, she was in the car. I drove for about 30 minutes in silence.

"Kendrick, if this isn't about work, I need to go back. I have a certain amount I need to make," she said.

"How much you make, or are supposed to make a day?" I asked, looking straight and continuing to drive.

"$6000."

"I'll give you 8," I replied, pulling over at one of my condos.

"$8000?!"

"Yeah. Don't trip," I said, shutting the engine off.

Once inside my condo, I gave her some juice and sat down across from her. "So this nigga French, I need you to tell me everything you know about him."

"Kendrick. He will kill me. I-"

"Nah ma. I got you. Who you trust more, him or me?" I asked, flashing a smile.

She blushed. "You."

"Good. Now talk to me."

She told me how he planned to kidnap Nic and her friends, to put on the track. She told me he was prepping Danielle to get closer to Nic so he could slither into our operation. I was mad as hell by the time she was done.

"Are you mad at me?" she asked, noticing my facial expression.

Tia was a pretty girl. Very fair-skinned, but you could tell she was black; full lips, curly hair, and skinny. She reminded me of Jurnee Smollett. I felt bad for her, cause she was way too sweet to be caught up in this shit. She reminded me of a dumb, weak, more slutty version of Nic. It's nicer than it sounds, trust me.

"Nah I'm not mad at you, Tia," I said, making her smile.

She stood up and began undressing. "Whoa Tia! What you doing?" I said putting, my hand up. I was horny as fuck, but not that horny.

"I wanted to thank you for the money," she said, almost in a whisper.

"Nah, no need. The $8000 was for the info. But you not going back to French," I peeled off the $8000 for her. "Here, keep this as money to have in case you need something. You gon' stay with my boy Jules for a bit, until we body French."

"I can't stay with you?"

"Tia, nah. You know I'm in a relationship with Nic, and that wouldn't look good."

"I see. I didn't know that. She told her mother, who told my mother, that she was pretty much done with you."

That shit made my heart physically hurt, but as long as she had my son and new baby in her stomach, she wasn't done with nothing.

"Tia, still-"

"I feel safer with you!" she cut me off.

"Okay. Okay, but no more stripping for me and shit."

"Okay," she smiled.

"You hungry?" I asked her. She shook her head yes, and I took her to get some lunch.

I knew I shouldn't have said yes to her staying with me, but she looked so fucking sad. I wasn't dumb though, I let her stay at one of the condos I barely used, so I knew she'd be safe there. I had Dice look after her and watch for any suspicious shit when I wasn't visiting.

Chapter Seven: Danielle Moore

Since Tia disappeared, French had been acting crazy as hell. Tia was supposed to be my girl, and for her to leave me here like this let me know she would rather be an enemy. French had us working the streets for a while now, and having her with me made me a bit stronger. When we first me French, I had no problem doing whatever he wanted, because I thought I was that bitch. Right now, I'm wishing I could turn back time, and be able to chill with my auntie and Nic while watching TV again. As much as I hated Nic, I missed her and my aunt Mariah. I thought about texting her, but I knew she would tell my aunt where I was, and I didn't want French to hurt them. Every time I told him I couldn't get info from Nic about Kendrick, he fucked me up. In reality, I hadn't even attempted to contact her for her safety.

French wouldn't let me leave his sight, unless it was to work the block or "see Nic." If I did try to escape, he would find me and fuck me up. Trust me, Tia and I tried it, and we didn't make it two blocks before he caught up with us. I wasn't sure how Tia got away, and neither was French. He looked high and low for her everyday, and each day he didn't find her, he whooped my ass. We recruited another girl by the name of Kimmy, and she was pretty cool. I was just happy to have someone else here to take a percentage of these beatings with me. Surprisingly, French let me keep my phone, and I would text July and Paris here and there just to update them on my situation. Gina never responded, so I stopped trying. I made them believe everything was peaches and cream, and that French was the love of my life. I did ask them if they'd seen Tia around, but they said no.

French and I arrived to his home that he swore was ours, but it didn't feel like home to me.

"It's 6pm, you should probably start getting ready," he told me. I wanted to break down and cry so badly, but I needed to be strong. This was the life I asked for, so I needed to be a woman about it. "Hey, where is my kiss?" he asked, yanking my arm hard as hell.

"Ouch!" I yelped.

He planted a kiss on my lips and grabbed my ass. I wanted to throw up, but I held it in for my face's sake. "I love you girl!" he yelled after me as I went into the bathroom.

I cut the shower on and began to remove my clothes. I cried silently as I looked in the wide mirror across the wall. I was no longer the girl I once was. I no longer wanted to only be wifey to a boss nigga. Right now, a man that loved me for me was good enough, no matter what his pockets looked like. I wish I had hung around my cousin, instead of girls with a mindset that was just as tainted as mine. I bit my lip to keep from making a sound, and let the tears fall. I got in the shower and let the water soothe the bruises from my constant ass whippings. Once I was dressed in my short red dress and stilettos to match, I was ready to start work. I sprayed some Victoria's Secret Bombshell perfume, then headed out the door.

"Sup ma?" a nice looking guy pulled on the side of me. I thanked God in my head, because I was tired of these ugly niggas.

"Hey," I said, attempting to smile.

"Get in," he instructed, and reached across his passenger seat to open the door for me.

I slid into his Lexus truck, and the heated seats soothed my bruised body. "What are you looking to get tonight?" I asked, hopping straight to the point.

"Full service," he said, making me roll my eyes.

I just wasn't in the mood to do much right now, and my body was in pain. I hated my damn life, but at least he was cute as fuck. He pulled over in a dark area to park his car. He seemed too young to be wanting or needing to pay for sex. He had to be about 19 years old. "What's your name, ma?" he asked me.

"Danielle."

"That's a pretty name Danielle, I'm Damien," he said smiling.

He was super cute, brown-skinned, had a pretty smile, and a low fade. "Thank you, and nice to meet you too."

We climbed into the backseat, and he began to remove my dress from my body. He touched my bruises, and I winced in pain. He leaned over and kissed my lips, making me pull back.

"Why did you do that?" I asked.

"Do what?"

"Kiss me?"

"Cause I wanted to. I'm paying aren't I?"

"Yeah, but kissing is an intimate thing."

"Charge me extra," he said before leaning over and kissing me hard.

His lips felt like heaven, and I melted. He unhooked my bra and started to lick and suck on my nipples. I took off his shirt and started to unbuckle his pants. I took him into my mouth, and he moaned softly. I glided up and down his shaft, making sure he touched my tonsils. He put his fingers in my hair and guided me up and down his penis. He pulled me up and removed my panties. He pushed me back and kissed my lips again. He kissed from my stomach to my pussy, making sure to kiss each bruise on the way down. No John had ever went down on me, and I didn't expect them to. He started to lick and suck my clit hard, making me cry out. He dipped his tongue in my hole and started to finger me. I came all over his fingers, and he slid a condom onto his dick. He entered me, and his big dick felt like it was ripping me open. Thank God French hadn't touched me in weeks, and my past clients were small in that department.

"Fuck ma. This shit is good as fuck!" he moaned as he rammed into me.

We soon exploded together, and he tongued kissed me passionately. I didn't know what his deal was, but I hoped to see him again.

"Take my number and let me know when that nigga put his hands on you again," he said as he started up his car. I stored his number and he gave me $4000.

"You only owe me $200," I told him.

"Nah, I don't want you working no more tonight." He leaned in and kissed me again before I got out. I didn't know who he was, but I wanted to find out. I smiled as I looked at his name stored in my phone.

Chapter Seven: Tia Alexander

Happy was an understatement. I had been living with the love of my life for weeks now, with no Nic in sight. That whole *she told my mother this* bullshit was just that–bullshit. I would stay up as late as I could waiting for Kendrick to come home to the condo we shared. I would even sleep in his shirts to smell his cologne. Sometimes he wouldn't come home, but I knew it was because he was busy handling business. We slept in two different rooms, but tonight I was gonna make my move on him.

I overheard him on the phone with Nic, so I put my ear to the room door since he had her on speaker. He must've assumed I was sleep, because he never put her on speaker, and he called her ass every night he was here.

"Nic, baby I just want to talk to you."

"About what Kendrick?" she asked sadly.

"Just come to me and you will find out. Or I can come to you, babe. Please. You got me begging and I don't beg." I rolled my eyes.

"No, because soon as I see you, you gon' convince me to come back and I can't do that until you commit. Fully."

"Nic, I miss you baby girl. I need you, you can't do me like this."

"Stop saying that you need me, Kendrick. I know what you trying to do," she said, crying like the weak ass bitch she was.

"But I do baby. And you need me, I just want to hold you," he said in a low tone. This nigga was cup-caking and simping like a muthafucka. "I miss you Nic. I'm dying without you, girl."

"Kendriiiiccckkkk," she whined through tears. *Ughck!*

"You carrying my baby, Nic. I need you and KJ at home with me. Please. Don't you love me and need me too?" *Please say no*, I thought. I was a little bothered to hear she was pregnant again.

"You know I do, Kendrick. I love you too much, and that's the problem."

"Then come to daddy." She just kept crying and crying, annoying the fuck out of me.

"Kendrick I hav…have to go," she stuttered through tears, and hung up. *Thank God!*

"Fuck!" he yelled, and it sounded like he threw his phone into the wall.

I ran into the bathroom just in time, cause I heard his bedroom door open. He turned on the TV in the living room, and I walked out in my bra and panties. It was dark except for the light from the TV. He looked over at me in my bra and panties, and exhaled heavily in frustration. I walked over to him slowly and sat next to him. He looked from the TV, smirked at me, and turned back. I saw "Nic Amyah" tatted on his neck and rolled my eyes. He opened a family sized bag of chips, and started crunching on them. He pointed the bag towards me to offer me some, and I shook my head no. I grabbed his face, inhaled his cologne, and kissed his cheek, making him move away. He kept his eyes on the TV.

"Kendrick, why don't you like me?" I asked.

He rested his arm in the chip bag and exhaled. "I do like you," he finally responded as he started back eating the chips and watching "Booty Call."

"No. Like me like you liked Paris," I said as he laughed at Jamie Foxx.

"I never liked Paris. I liked her pussy and head game," he chuckled at his own half joke, and reached for his glass of water for a drink. He didn't once take his eyes off the TV.

"Well how come you don't like mine?" I asked boldly, staring at the side of his face.

He gulped down the water and sat it back down. "Okay, so you want to suck my dick and let me fuck you, then what? We gon' be together?" He finally looked at me and raised an eyebrow. He chuckled and looked back at the TV. He was so sexy.

"I don't know. I just want to feel you."

He put down his chips on the coffee table, and reached one hand behind me to unsnap my bra with ease. He bit his lip and yanked my panties down while keeping eye contact with me. He rubbed up my thighs and spread them. I inhaled deeply and started to tense up, because I was nervous as fuck. He rubbed his hands between my breasts and down my stomach, making me jump a little. I was so nervous I couldn't think straight.

"That's why I don't like you like that, you don't even know what to do with a nigga like me. You scared for me to even touch you. Dick can't even get hard with the way you jumping and flinching," he smirked in an irritated fashion, grabbed his chips, and started back eating them while watching TV.

I couldn't believe I fucked this up. I waited years to fuck him, and I bitched up in the moment. I went to the room I slept in and cried myself to sleep.

Chapter Seven: Jessica Leon

"So Ms. Leon, you are definitely pregnant, but you're not too far along for an abortion like you asked. Is that something you still want to do?" Fuck my life. I loved Kendon, but we were not stable enough to have a baby.

"Yes, how does it work?'

"Well the best way for you to do this if you'd like to have children in the future, is to take a pill that will pretty much flush the baby out of you. You will bleed a lot, because you're having an abortion, but it's best for someone of your age."

"Okay, will I need someone to drive me or anything?" I asked, scared as fuck.

"No, you can take the pill home with you. Then once you get home, you can take it there. Just make sure you have plenty of sanitary napkins, preferably the ones for a heavy flow," she half smiled.

"Okay well yes, I will do that, Dr. Keen," I exhaled heavily.

***

I arrived home and went straight to the bathroom. I thanked God that Kendon was not home, so I could hurry and take this pill. I grabbed some water and prepared to take it. I stopped and looked at myself in the mirror to make sure this is what I wanted at the moment. I thought about how much Kendon and I fight, and knew it was best for the baby that it not even come in contact with us. I popped the pill in my mouth and swallowed. I placed a pad in my underwear and decided to take a nap.

***

"Jessica, get up baby!" I woke up to Kendon yelling.

I sat up and saw blood everywhere, and my sheets were drenched. "Oh my gosh! Fuck!" I yelled as I clenched my stomach, due to the overwhelming pain.

"Babe what the fuck is going on?!" Kendon yelled as he stared down at me in terror. I knew if I told him, he might murder me.

"I'm having a miscarriage, Kendon!" I cried. Actual tears were flowing from my eyes due to the pain I was in, and the fact that I had actually killed my baby.

"You were pregnant?!" he asked, looking confused.

"Yeah, I just found out," I told him as I sat up slowly.

"Come on ma, let's go to the emergency. This is a lot of blood!" he yelled, helping me off the bed.

"No Kendon, can we not! I'm embarrassed. I just want to clean this blood off me. Please," I cried and dropped onto the floor.

Thank God he said okay, and went to run me a bath. When I got in, he went to make me some food, and I cried as I soaked my body. I was in so much pain and was bleeding profusely. The doctor told me ahead of time I would bleed a lot, and be in some pain for about two days, so I didn't feel the need to visit a hospital. There was no way in hell I could ever tell Kendon what I had done. I'm pretty sure our already strained relationship would be over for good. Now that I'm thinking about it, I wish I had never done it. I acted way too quickly and I was now regretting it.

After my bath, I ate the baked chicken and rice that he made me. Afterwards, we retired to bed and I started to doze off. I woke up in the middle of the night and heard Kendon sobbing quietly in the bathroom, located in our room. That shit broke my heart into pieces. I got out of bed and opened the bathroom door. Kendon picked his head up out of his hands, and his face was wet with tears. I walked up to him, and he grabbed me by my waist and hugged me tightly. He pressed his head against my stomach. He drenched my shirt in tears as he broke down. I wrapped my arms around him and caressed his head. Seeing him like this made me cry as well. I hated myself; sometimes I was so selfish, and never thought about other people. I hurt the one nigga that actually loved and cared about me, and I wanted to turn back time more than anything.

Chapter Seven: Nic Fuller

I was missing Kendrick like crazy, but I needed to be strong. I had been checking his Instagram, but his last post was when he announced I was pregnant with KJ over a year ago.

Kayden was out of town for a small tour he was on, so Christy and I decided to go out. I hadn't been out in awhile, so I couldn't wait, even though this baby had me sick already. Some basketball player who just got drafted was celebrating at King Brother's. I didn't want to go, but Christy assured me that Kendrick and his brothers rarely hung out with the crowd, so it was unlikely that I'd see him.

I had on jean shorts, and a quarter-sleeve black sheer button up, that stopped right where my shorts did. I had on some thigh high Tom Ford sandal heels. My dark hair was pressed with a part down the middle, and stopped right at the middle of my back. Of course, my makeup was the natural nude look; my signature. I sprayed my Marc Jacobs Daisy perfume, and headed outside. I thought about taking my necklace off that had the initial K on it, but changed my mind. Plus, my son was Kendrick as well!

"You look sexyyyyy!" Christy beamed when I got in the car.

She was the only one I told about what Michael did, and what Kendrick did to him. I was gon' tell the other girls, but I was still slightly embarrassed to, especially with Jessica. When I told Christy, she cried so hard and it caught me off guard. Before Kendrick, Christy was always my protector. I didn't need her to be, but she naturally did so. If you said anything to me, Christy would fuck you up before I could even respond. That's how it was, Christy was the *no talking just fight*-fighter, Jessica was the *smart mouth* fighter, Morgan was the *optimistic sweetheart but will still fuck you up* fighter, and I was the *quiet and cool until you push me* fighter.

"Thank you. So do you," I smiled.

Her brownish blonde hair was in its naturally curly state, and she had on red lipstick. She wore an Africa print red dress that dipped super low in the front, stopping right under her belly button. She had on sandal stilettos in black. We looked real good. She drove to KB's, and we danced to "Truffle Butter" by Nicki Minaj on the way there.

We arrived, and the line was out the fucking door. I shook my head, cause I did not want to stand in line. I wasn't sure if Kendrick had let them know we wasn't together or not. We walked up slowly about to ask how much to get in.

"Mrs. King," the bouncer smiled at me and removed the line separator. "Enjoy ladies," he continued before we could even say anything.

I turned around, shrugged at Christy, and we laughed. The music was jumping loud as hell as usual. These two girls were on stage dancing to "Bitch Better Have My Money" by Rihanna. I'd much rather see men, but we had to be 21 for that. Christy and I started dancing and singing the lyrics with each other. I was having so much fun until I spotted Kendrick in a VIP booth laughing and talking with his brothers, plus Jules, Damien, Ricky, and Maurice. It was a gang of bitches sitting there too. My stomach instantly felt queasy at the sight of him enjoying himself without me. Then Paris hoe ass came out on stage, dancing to "No Type" by Rae Sremmurd. Niggas was cheering and clapping for her. I rolled my eyes hard as hell.

"You good?' Christy asked.

She was the only one I told that Kendrick cheated, and Morgan. Jessica would kill me if she knew what I was keeping from her, but I didn't want her saying she told me so. She was an Aquarius, so she thought she knew everything. Morgan was a Gemini, so that's why she was half-sweet and half-street. Christy was a feisty Leo, and I'm a laid back Sagittarius.

"Yeah I'm okay," I responded, keeping my eyes on Kendrick.

He couldn't see me cause of the crowd of people where I was. He and his friend's eyes were glued to Paris as she danced seductively to the song, sliding up and down the pole, flipping upside down, and making her ass clap. While sipping his drink, Kendrick, his brothers, and his boys were cheesing hard at this hoe as she tore up the stage. Christy and I decided to sit down, and I made sure it was a table where I had good view of this nigga.

"What's up with y'all anyway Nic?" Christy frowned as we sat down.

"I don't even know. He be acting like he wants me back, but that's not how it's looking to me," I frowned as I played with my "K" chain.

"Nic, he is out with his friends. What, you want him to be sulking and blowing up your phone?" Christy smiled.

"No...but damn. He look like he is happy as hell," I said as I watched him light up a blunt. He was just having a funky good time with his bitch ass.

Paris finished her set, came down, and walked her weak ass straight over to my nigga; broken up or not, he was my nigga. She walked into the booth, and sat right next to Kendrick. He poured her a drink, and handed it to her as he laughed with Jules and Maurice. She draped her arm over his shoulder, and leaned her head on his shoulder. I was pissed the fuck off. I don't care if we wasn't together, I warned this bitch! Christy gave me a look saying she was down if I wanted to get at this hoe. Paris kissed his cheek, and nuzzled her face in his neck. He was so high and drunk, he didn't even realize it–I hoped. She draped her leg over his, and he quickly moved it off. She just laid her head back on his shoulder. That was it; I had to take my ass over there!

"Be right back, Christy."

"Nic! You don't want me to come?"

"Nah I'm good."

I walked up as he and his boys were singing the words to "6 God" by Drake. I stood there and folded my arms. Kendrick continued to laugh and talk, while this bitch sipped her drink with her head on his shoulder, like they was a couple. I wanted to see just how out of it this nigga was. Jules finally noticed me, and tapped his shoulder. Kendrick looked over at me, and his smile faded quick as fuck.

"Nic," was all his dumb ass could say.

He had on jeans, a dark grey hoodie, and Jordans. Some random stripper bitch had his hat on. *The fuck?!* At least he had on his small, gold "N" chain. Paris' head shot up off his shoulder, and Kendrick rushed down the five little steps, to me.

"Baby girl, what you doing here?" he asked, looking scared as hell and grabbing my waist.

"Just enjoying myself, like you," I fake smiled, keeping my arms folded and leaning back, still in his embrace.

"Nic, it's not even like that," he said, looking back over his shoulder and rubbing my lower back.

"Then what the fuck is it like? Is this what you do every night? Hug up with a bitch, then go home and fill my ear with bullshit about how you missing me?" I raised my eyebrow.

"I do miss you babe, I just…ah…" he said, rubbing his hand over his face and licking his lips. He was so fucking cross-faded it was ridiculous. His green eyes were glossy as hell. He looked sexy as fuck with his drunk, high ass. He pursed his lips, making his sexy dimples appear.

"You don't fucking miss me. You miss this," I pointed to the strippers in his booth. "That's what you miss. Fucking random hoes, and getting drunk and high!" I finished.

"Nic, I been going out of my way to get you back to me, but you not giving me nothing. What, you want me to sit and wait?" he frowned and shrugged.

"No, I don't Kendrick. Don't wait at all," I said and started to walk away, because I didn't want him to know I was about to cry. I swear, being pregnant makes you a damn crybaby. I hated his ass!

He grabbed my arm and put his other one around my shoulder, bringing me in close to his face. His cologne smelled so good; I missed his scent. He wiped the single tear on my face with his thumb, and kissed my lips.

"You need to relax. You're pregnant. You know I love you, stop acting like that," he said in a low tone as he looked me in my face.

I instantly got wet and wanted to feel him inside me so bad. He kissed my lips again, and I lightly pushed him off, making him give up. I started to walk off, then stopped. I turned around and saw him walking back up the five little stairs to his booth. I followed right behind him and punched Paris, who was now standing, dead in her face. She fell on the table, and broke the glasses that were resting on it. Before she could even get her hoe ass up, I walked off.

"Let's go Christy!" I yelled.

Christy walked fast after me, while trying to see what the commotion was by Kendrick's booth.

Chapter Eight: Kendrick King

Making Tia think I lived there, trying to save Danielle, trying to get Nic back, and protecting and running a business had a nigga stressing hard. Ever since Tia tried to push up on me that night, and I scared her ass off, she'd been acting 100. I was happy, cause if she pushed up on me once more, I was gon' have to pack her shit and put her with Jules like I originally planned.

I just knew gray hair was coming in, which is why I was happy when Kendon decided to throw a little backyard BBQ. I walked in with Tia, and everybody was there except Morgan and Dreeis, since she just gave birth a couple weeks ago. I looked around for Nic, but then stopped. I needed to stop acting like a bitch for her, and handle my fucking business. Ever since she came over that day, and I almost had her, she refused to see me. I hadn't seen her in a month and a half after that night at KB's. She barely took my calls, and never texted me back.

"Mr. King, long time no see!"

I turned to see Honey's fine ass, and my dick got hard immediately. I hadn't had any type of action in forever.

"What's up Honey?" I smiled.

"You still fine as ever daddy." I sat down on the bench that Kendon had set up, and she sat in my lap. I didn't protest. I was a single, horny man. She rubbed her small hands through my short curly fro, and licked her lips.

"You gon' finally give me a taste?"

"Taste of what?" I smiled. I had let her suck my dick, but I didn't fuck, so I guess that's what she wanted.

"Some dick," she leaned down to whisper.

Just as she did, I saw Nic walk into the backyard where everyone was. She had on an off the shoulder crop top, tight jeans, and sandals. Her beautiful skin glowed, and she had that same some up some down style as last time. Her ass was super fat in the jeans she had on, and my dick was on brick status.

"Kendrick!" Honey yelled, snapping me out my trance.

Nic shook her head in disappointment, then walked over to hug her friends. I continued to flirt with Honey, and Nic kept glancing over. I rubbed up Honey's thick thighs while she was in my lap.

"One second," I said, sliding her off my lap. I needed to get Nic back, cause there was no way I could watch her be with another nigga. I followed Nic into the kitchen of Kendon's condo.

"Why you acting like that? And where is my son?" I said, grabbing her arm and bringing her in close.

"Move Kendrick, you make me sick. KJ is at my mom's," she spat, moving me off her. She started looking over the food that was there and pulled out two plates, making me laugh.

"It must be a boy, cause you eating a lot," I said, putting my hand on her tummy. I was starting to see a bulge, but it was still flat.

"Don't touch me," she said softly, slapping my hand away.

I put my hand around her waist, and took the plate out of her hand. "Kendrick, give me my food," she whined.

I sat it on the table and put my other hand around her body, pulling her in. I planted soft kisses on her lips, and she didn't resist. I dipped my tongue in her mouth, and we kissed hard as hell. I squeezed her ass and she moaned in my mouth. I wanted to fuck her right on the kitchen floor.

"Kendrick!" Honey yelled from outside. *Fuck.*

Nic pulled away from my grasp. "Go tend to your bitch, nigga." She grabbed her plate and stormed out.

I was tired of this shit. "It's a bedroom right here if you ready," I offered to Honey as I stood in the doorway of the backyard. I was horny as fuck, and I was about to fix that shit right now! She hopped up and switched her fat ass past me into the house. I followed, ignoring Nic's glances. I was tired of chasing her. She was gon' give a young player gray hair.

Once in the room, Honey took off her dress. Her body was bomb as hell–hips, ass, titties, damn! I still preferred Nic's body, though. She was slimmer, but had a nice small plump ass, perkier titties, more toned stomach, but not a six-pack or anything. I'm sure her pussy was tighter, too.

"Come here," I told her. She came over and kneeled down, unzipping my pants. Just as she started to tease the tip, I heard the door bust open.

"You got me fucked up, Kendrick!" Nic yelled as she pulled Honey by her hair and swung her onto the floor.

I put my dick away, scared as hell. Honey hopped up, swung, and missed. Nic started fucking her ass up bad as hell. The bitch was calling the Holy Trinity as she backed up, attempting to do the windmill. Dumb ass. When Nic flung her over the dresser, wiping off everything on it, I grabbed her Hulk ass. She was small as fuck, but fighting like a linebacker. I guess pregnancy made her stronger.

"Let me go nigga!" The first words she said to me when I first met her.

"I didn't then, and I'm not now." I carried her into the other room, and let her squirming ass down. I was laughing.

"What's so fucking funny, nigga?!"

"Cause as much as you don't want to admit it, you want to be back with me," I said, cracking up.

"No, I hate you."

"Then why you just fuck that girl up?" I said, moving closer to her and biting my lip.

"Cause. I'm pregnant with your baby, and I have your son, and you out here fucking her!"

"I didn't fuck her, Nic. I been begging you to see me for weeks, ma. What you want me to do?" I pleaded, taking her into my arms.

"I want you to want me like I want you, Kendrick!"

"What? I do! Why you think I went from being myself to Keith Sweat these past weeks, trying to get you home," I smiled, making her chuckle.

"No, I want you to want me as more than just your baby mama. I'm already having your second baby, and nothing from you."

"Babe, you have to trust me when I say I love you and my son more than anything, and I would never leave you like that. I want nothing more than to make you my wife, why you think I asked you? I just need you to stay down for me while I handle this shit, and then I promise as soon as this nigga is in the grave, I will make your crazy ass my wife," I smiled and kissed the back of her hands. "Okay?"

She shook her head yes. "Okay."

"You too pretty to be fucking hoes up, but that shit turned me on, ma."

"I missed you, Kendrick."

"Yeah I can tell."

"You still love me as much as before?" she asked.

"I never stopped." We were tonguing it up, and I pulled her top off. I ran back and locked the door. "I don't need no more bust ins." We both laughed.

Once naked, I kissed from her lips to her stomach, and kissed and licked all over it. I spread her legs and made love to her pussy with my mouth.

"Ahhhhh."

"What's my name?" I said in between licks.

"King Ken," she moaned out as she ran her fingers through my short, curly fro.

I continued to punish her shit with my tongue, licking and sucking and dipping my tongue in her hole. She tried to move up, but I had her bottom half on lock. Her legs started to tremble, and she came hard as fuck. I missed eating her pussy. I loved doing it period, but it was only for wifey. I flipped her over, and started licking and sucking on her pussy and her ass, making her scream out. She came again, and I slid into her from behind. I ran my hands down her back and smacked her ass. She was already sweating from me eating her.

"Whose pussy is this?" I moaned, ramming into her. It had been forever, and there was nothing like pregnant pussy. Shit was amazing.

"Yours Kendrick! AHHH!"

I smiled as I looked down at my full name "Kendrick Dreaux King" tatted on her lower back. I grabbed her hair, and fucked her hard as hell. She moved me back, and I fell onto the bed. She climbed on top of me, with her back turned to me. She started riding me backwards nice and slow. She was so wet that all you heard was my dick going in and out.

"Fuck ma!" she made me moan out as she sped up, making her ass jiggle.

"Kendrick baby," she moaned as she leaned back, putting her palms on my chest.

She started bouncing on my dick, making me want to scream like a little girl. She had a nigga gone off this pussy. *Fuck!* I sat up and put her back doggy style as I pounded her shit with force. She came all over my dick, and I spread her cheeks to get a good view of me killing the pussy. Her shit was so pretty. The sight of her small plump ass in my hands jiggling, and her tight pussy creaming on my dick right before my eyes, made me bust hard as fuck. I planted kisses down her sexy, sweaty back.

"Next weekend babe. Let's get married next weekend, but in Baltimore. We can honeymoon later in California," I offered.

"Anything you want, babe," she panted. "No, Paris. Honeymoon in Paris," she smiled.

"Paris it is," I smiled.

"And any bitch that tries to ride my dick is getting fucked up too," she glared.

I laughed and grabbed her wrist. I kissed her tattoo that said "Mrs. Kendrick King." She had K.D.K. behind her ear too. All these tattoos she had showing niggas what it was, turned me on. We showered and fucked two more times before returning to the party. Honey was gone; someone took her to the hospital. *Damn.* She just broke Paris' nose a month ago. My baby was getting reckless. Ha.

Chapter Eight: Danielle Moore

Damien became a regular of mine. I wouldn't see any other dudes, because he would always pay me enough to head back to the house with French. We would sometimes go eat food, just to make it seem more legit by stretching the time I was gone. French would be high as hell when I got there anyways, or laid up with a new girl he recruited. He hadn't put his hands on me since I met Damien, and I was happy, because Damien seemed to be a hot head and I knew he would run up on French ASAP.

I started dressing up even more, knowing that I was gonna see him. I walked to my normal spot that Damien picked me up at, and I smiled when I saw his car approaching. I hopped in and he turned to me for a kiss. "You hungry?" he asked, and I shook my head yes.

"You don't want to…you know, first?" I asked. I didn't want him to think I had gotten too comfortable.

"Nah, ma, I want to take you out. You look nice," he smiled as he pulled from the curb.

We arrived at this steakhouse that took us about 45 minutes to get to. My phone chimed, and it was a text from French; my heart dropped. I opened my phone and read it.

"You doing double time tonight. Kimmy is sick baby girl, and she can't go." I replied okay, and locked my phone.

French seemed to take a liking to Kimmy, and I was happy that she was now his bedmate and primary punching bag. "You good?" Damien asked, putting the menu down.

"Yeah perfect. Lucifer says I have to stay out later tonight," I smiled.

"Cool, more time we can be together," he said, touching my hand.

"What's that nigga's name for real?" he asked.

"I don't want to talk about him, Damien," I replied. I didn't want to tell him, because he might go after him. "What do you do for a living, Damien?" I asked, sipping my lemonade.

"Let's just say, freelance work," he said, flashing his perfect white smile. I blushed and turned After we ate lunch, we decided to go back to his condo and watch TV.

"You miss me when I'm not around you?" he asked.

"Yeah, even though you see me every day, I still miss you. I wish I could cuddle with you at night," I told him honestly.

"You do?" he asked, muting the TV. I shook my head yes, and he planted a soft kiss on my lips. "Why don't you stop working for that guy?"

"I can't, he will kill me."

"I will protect you," he told me. Tears started to well up in my eyes as I shook my head no. "Danielle. I got you ma," he said, smiling.

"Okay, just give me some time." He shook his head yes, as if to say okay. I didn't know how I was gon' get away from French. This made me hate Tia even more, because she did it without me.

"You my girl, aight?" he said, looking into my eyes and letting me know he was serious.

"I know. I haven't been seeing anyone but you, like you told me."

"Good. That pussy belongs to me now," he said as he dipped his tongue in my mouth.

He lifted my dress to my waist, and pulled my panties down. He put his head between my legs and worked his magic. I came all over his mouth, and he licked me clean like it was his last meal. He flipped me on all fours and entered me from behind. He pounded into me as he held my waist.

"Ahhhhhh!" I moaned out loud as he tore my shit up.

"Whose is it, Danielle?" he asked as I came all over his dick.

"Yours, Damien!" I yelled out just as he exploded into me.

He unzipped my dress to remove it fully, and we went for round two in his bedroom. I set my alarm for four hours and fell asleep in his embrace, like I've wanted to do this whole time.

Chapter Eight: Damien Kidd

I'm sure y'all wondering why I wifed a streetwalker. Danielle was the prettiest girl I had ever seen. She had flawless mocha skin, a banging body, and long, pretty, dark hair. She had dark brown eyes, and plump perfectly shaped lips, with a Marilyn Monroe mole above the top one. I first saw her when I pulled into a McDonalds to get some food, and she was walking by. I knew what she did for a living right away, but for some reason that didn't phase me. She had to have been new, because I knew all the hoes out here, and I'd never seen her. I watched the areas she stayed in, and decided to approach her one night. She was even more gorgeous up close, and I wanted her bad.

There was no way I was telling my boys about her, though; not until she stopped working the block. Once she deaded that selling pussy shit, I would bring her around my peoples. I just hoped she did it ASAP, because I was starting to have feelings for her, and the thought of her fucking for cash, or that nigga she worked for putting hands on her, had my blood boiling.

The first night I slept with her, she had so many bruises all over her perfect body, and that shit pissed me off–not even because I liked her, though. I hated for any woman to get beat on like that. I guess because my dad used to fuck my mother up, and one day he beat her into a coma that she didn't wake up from. Ever since then, I despised any nigga who put they hands on a female. I had it bad for Danielle, regardless of her choice of work, but I needed her to know I was serious about her leaving that shit in the past.

I had went and purchased a diamond promise ring for her; just a little something to solidify our relationship. I pulled up to our normal meeting spot, and she got in the car.

"Sup ma," I said, pulling from the curb.

"Hey," she said, attempting to smile, but I could tell she was sad. I peeped a bruise where her neck and collarbone met, pissing me off.

"Danielle. You not going back," I said, attempting to contain my anger.

"Dame I have to! I told you I need some time to figure everything out!" she yelled, with tears running down her beautiful face.

"It's either this shit or me!" I spat, pulling over.

"Damien, I told you-"

"Get out the car!" I cut her ass off.

"What I-"

"Get out the fucking car!" I yelled, mad as hell.

She hopped out the car and I sped off, leaving her standing there. After driving for about five minutes, I just couldn't get her sad face out my mind after leaving her there. I made a U-turn, and drove until I saw her walking. A guy approached her, and I parked my car and hopped out.

"Shop is closed," I told him before taking her hand in mine and leading her to my car. I opened the door for her, and she slid into my whip.

"You came back, why?" she said, folding her arms as I drove off.

"Because I'm taking you to my crib, and that's where you gon' stay. You done with this shit, and I mean that Danielle." She didn't say anything.

We arrived to my crib, and I led her to my room.

"I got this for you," I said, pulling a Versace dress and matching shoes from my closet.

"Thank you baby! What's the occasion?" she asked, smiling big.

"I want to take you on a nice dinner date," I smiled, admiring her pretty face.

Tears began to well up as she planted a kiss on my lips. We showered together, and I took her to The Prime Rib.

"This is so good, I've never had anything this fancy in my life," she beamed.

"Well, I'm happy to be your first," I said as I slid a blue velvet box across the table.

She stopped eating and looked at me as she grabbed it.

"What's this?" she asked with a slight smile.

"Open it," I told her, anxious for her to see it.

"Damien!" she yelped as she slid it on her finger. "What's this for?"

"Just to let you know I'm serious about you." She looked down at it smiling, and I peeped that bruise on her collarbone again. I got pissed again, so I had to shake the thoughts from my mind to enjoy the night.

"Thank you, Dame," she said slightly, getting out of her seat for a kiss, and I gave her one.

"I dig you, ma."

"I dig you too, baby," she smirked.

We continued to enjoy the night with conversation and food. When we got home, we made love all night. Whether Danielle wanted to tell me or not, I was gon' find out who her pimp was and kill his ass.

Chapter Nine: Morgan Garrett

Flashback - 5 Weeks Ago

I was in labor, and it was the worst pain ever. Kendreeis was there holding my hand, and my mom was sitting there with tears in her eyes. Finally, after 13 hours of labor, our son Kaleeini Drake King was born, and he was so cute. We decided against naming him Kendreeis, because there was already a KJ in the family; he had Dreeis' middle name, though. He had super curly hair and those signature King man green eyes; I guess their eyes were a dominant gene.

Everybody was in the room looking at him, and saying how cute he was. I loved him so much already. Baby Kendrick kept staring with his little eyes bucked; I guess he hadn't seen too many other babies. Nic and I were best friends, and now our babies were cousins, crazy how life turns out.

***

Present Time

Kaleeini had been home with us for about five weeks now, and he was perfect. He didn't cry much, except for when he was sleepy or needed changing. It was a little harder than I thought it would be, taking care of him and making sure I kept up with my homework assignments. I was taking classes at Morgan State, but online like Nic. I thought it would be easier, but it seems since you don't have to go to class, they give you much more homework. Then on top of that, Dreeis stayed out late as hell all the damn time, trying to get this nigga named French. He didn't want me out because the guy planned to kidnap Christy, Nic, Jessica, and myself for his ho stroll; I'll be damned if he had my ass working the stroll. Fuck out of here. However, no matter how tough I thought I was, Kendreeis wasn't having it.

While Kaleeini slept, I finished the quesadillas and homemade chips and salsa I was making for dinner. I already knew to put my baby's up, cause he wouldn't be here to eat with me I'm sure. Nic was coming over so we could catch up and eat, and I couldn't wait. Right when I finished setting the food up in the dining room, I heard the doorbell ring and a smile spread across my face.

"Hey sexy!" Nic beamed when I opened the door.

"Sexy? I don't feel sexy at all!" I frowned as she walked in.

Although my body was back it like it never left, I never really dressed up anymore, and I felt like a bum. Kaleeini spit up on my clothes a lot, so I didn't like wearing my good stuff. I just had on jeans, a white loose fitting layered spaghetti strap top, two long French braids, and magenta lipstick.

Christy and Jessica, decided they were going to go out despite Kayden and Kendon telling them not to; Nic and I knew better.

"Aww, you will soon enough," she smiled. We sat down and started eating the food.

"So how are your classes?" I asked, putting hot sauce on my quesadilla.

"Pretty cool. Some are really hard, and stressing me out. That period where I was away from Kendrick and had to watch KJ alone, plus do homework was just stressful as fuck. Then I'm carrying baby number two," she half smiled.

"Damn. I know what you mean." I shook my head at the thought. I couldn't imagine doing what I was doing right now and being pregnant. Even though she wasn't too far along, it still made you tired.

"What about yours?" she asked, chewing the chips.

I exhaled heavily, "It's been a lot, and then Kendreeis is never here to help me with the baby. I literally only see him after like 2 am when he sliding in the bed cuddling behind me. Is Kendrick out that late?" I asked, hoping she said yes.

"Yeah sometimes, it's frustrating," she replied.

Thank God, cause if Kendreeis was pretending to be handling business until two and three in the morning, I would be furious and a whole bunch of other shit.

We finished eating, and decided to watch Married to Medicine. When it was done, we decided to channel surf before resorting to Netflix. We arrived to the news channel, and stopped immediately.

"Promising basketball star Michael Lodenn, has been missing for months now. Lodenn was attending Morgan State University on a basketball scholarship, and

had many NBA teams interested in him. He went missing months ago, and has yet to be discovered," the newscaster said.

Nic and I watched as video footage of Michael playing in his college games played. We were stunned, but I couldn't help but notice I was a bit more stunned than her.

"A couple months before Lodenn's disappearance, his mother says he was seeing a therapist for depression. Apparently, he had broken up with his long time girlfriend, and it seemed to take a toll on him. His parents say that he began displaying unusual behavior, like not showing up to practices, games, family dinners, and staying out until all hours of the morning. Police are suspecting that Lodenn committed suicide in a location unfamiliar to his loved ones. His apartment showed no signs of a break in or kidnapping. Our prayers are with Mr. Lodenn's family. It would be such a loss to Morgan State and the NBA league as well, if he isn't found. Lodenn is 20 years old," the newscaster finished and pursed her lips. I cut the TV off and looked at Nic, who refused to look at me.

"Nic."

"Okay, okay. Some months back, Michael kidnapped me, beat me, and raped me," she finally spoke up, looking me in my eyes.

"What! What the fuck Nic?! When wa-" I chimed in, cutting her off.

"Wait, Morgan! It was while Kendrick was in a coma. When he woke up, he went after him and killed him," she said, looking down.

"Why didn't you tell me, Nic?" I asked with tears welling up. I couldn't believe this happened to her, and to know she was all alone broke my heart. I scooted closer to her so she could lay her head on my shoulder.

"I knew you would tell Dreeis, and he would've killed Michael. I wanted to do it on my own, but Kendrick woke up unexpectedly, and demanded to know what happened to my face. When I told him, he literally snatched the IV out his arm, and went after him," she cried and chuckled a bit.

"It's okay Nic. I'm sorry this happened to you," I said, shaking my head and smiling at the thought of Kendrick's crazy ass. This nigga Michael was out of his fucking mind. It's crazy how you never really know people.

We sat and talked for the rest of the night, until Kendreeis came home and she left. Dreeis had Dice follow her home. I couldn't believe what happened to her and it made me so sad.

"Home early, I see," I said as I put the food away.

"Don't start," was all he said, and went upstairs.

I finished putting up the food, and went upstairs to the bedroom. He wasn't in there, so I knew he was in the room with Kaleeini. I changed into my pajamas, and turned the TV on in the room. Thirty minutes later, he walked into the room and went straight to shower. What the fuck? Only reason he is showering is cause he just fucked a bitch! I was so mad waiting for him to get out that my leg was shaking.

After what seemed like forever, he walked out in just boxers with his dreads were down. He was so gorgeous. His sexy light caramel skin glistened, and his abs were perfectly etched in his abdomen. I could see his dick print through his boxers, and it made my mouth water.

"What you watching?" he asked, putting lotion on his strong arms and standing in front of the TV.

Fuck the lala, "Are you cheating on me? Just be honest, please," I said, getting straight to the point.

"What?!" he said, turning around frowning. His green eyes darkened in color. They were like mood rings, telling me he was slightly upset.

"Are. You. Chea-ting. On. Me," I said slowly since he was hard of fucking hearing. I cut the TV off, cause I needed to hear this loud and clear.

"Hell nah, I'm not! I've never cheated on you during this whole relationship, why would I start now?" he said, smiling and showing his perfect white teeth. I was gon' fuck him before I left if he was cheating, that's for sure.

"You always out late as fuck! And then now you hopped in the shower soon as you got here!" I said, trying to hold back tears. This shit always happened. Stuff would be good, and then nigga's got tired of you, and started fucking around. This is exactly why I didn't want a relationship. All these niggas was the same.

He exhaled heavily, and walked over to me. He sat down and put my feet in his lap to massage them. He always did that when I was pregnant, and I loved it.

"Morgan, calm down baby. I have no reason to cheat on you, nor do I want to. I just asked you to marry me, and we just had a baby. I'm happy as hell right now," he said, looking into my eyes. "Ma, I promised you the first time we hung out, I would never do you like that," he continued.

I finally let the tears fall, while staring at him to see if he was lying. "Let me see your phone," I said sternly.

He paused and bit his lip, "You lucky I love your ass," he finally said, and got up to get me his phone. "Give me a kiss, and I will give it to you," he said, standing over me with his phone in his hand as I was sitting on the bed. I didn't respond, and he leaned down to kiss my lips. I moved a bit, and he landed on half of my mouth and half of my cheek. He laughed and handed it to me.

I looked in his phone, and went straight to his texts messages as he sat my feet back in his lap to massage them. I saw some from Kendrick, Kendon, Kayden, Jules, Maurice, Ricky, and Damien. I then saw some from Candace's wack ass, some bitch named Ivy, Lisa, and another chick named Tamia, but they all had no responses from him. Thank God. I checked his call log and pretty much saw the same thing. These bitches calling him knowing he has a family pissed me off.

Luckily they were in red, meaning he didn't answer. I checked his Instagram DM, and it was full of unread messages. I clicked on one and saw a pussy shot. *What the fuck!* But that's what my ass gets. I quickly hit the home button and clicked his email icon, and it took me to setup.

"You don't have email?" I frowned.

"Hell nah, fuck I need an email for?" he smiled, still massaging my feet.

I broke into tears, feeling dumb as hell. "I'm sorry Kendreeis! I know you're tired of me acting like this. It's just I'm not used to things going good like this for so long. I'm sorry, babe, I promise I'm not gonna act like this no more. It's just with me just having the baby, and you being gone all the time, I thought you didn't love me anymore," I sobbed, embarrassed as fuck.

He stopped massaging my feet, and pulled me into his lap.

"Don't cry ma, I understand. But it's the opposite. After the baby, I'm more in love with you. I don't like being away from you all night, but I have to in order to protect you and your friends. I can't let this nigga get y'all. He is giving us a run for our fucking money right now. He's killed a couple of our people, has robbed a couple houses, and we can't seem to find him. So I'm sorry babe that I'm gone, and haven't helped you with the baby much, but I'm gonna try to wake up earlier, so we can have more time together before I leave. I need to balance this shit, especially if I'm gonna be your husband one day," he said, looking in my eyes with his fine ass.

"I'm sorry baby. No, don't worry about me and Kaleeini right now, just do what you have to do," I smiled. I didn't want to stress him out. I didn't realize it was so much shit happening with him. I felt like a bitch for pressing him.

"Nah that's not an option. I'm gonna do better. I love you and Kaleeini, and I want to make sure I make you happy like I promised you I would. Plus you've made me so happy by agreeing to be my wife, having my son, and being able to cook, clean, and be in school. I love you with yo perfect ass," he smiled, biting his lip. His emerald eyes sparkled and lightened up. I knew that meant he was happy.

I laughed and he wiped my tears. "I love you too, Kendreeis." He dipped his tongue in my mouth and removed my pajama top. "

You look just as good as before," he said, eyeing my body.

He turned me over onto my back, and removed my pajama shorts and underwear. He climbed in between my legs and kissed me hard. He kissed my neck and collarbone. He stopped at my breasts, and sucked on my nipples while cupping my breasts. He kissed in between them, and trailed his tongue all the way down to my belly button. He stuck his tongue in my belly button and bit my flat stomach. I chuckled a bit, cause it tickled. I loved when he did that shit. He looked up at me and smiled, then continued to kiss my body with his soft lips.

"Ahh," I moaned softly, arching my back.

He planted kisses all the way down and lifted my leg. He planted more kisses on my inner thighs, then dived into my pussy. He flicked his tongue over, and sucked on my clit hard. He pushed my legs back, and licked and sucked every part of my shit. He dipped his tongue in my hole, and I came hard all over his mouth. He continued as if I hadn't.

"Daddy, you so good at this," I moaned, propping myself up on my elbows to get a good view.

He didn't say a word as he made me cum again. I hopped up and pushed him on the bed. I planted kisses down his chiseled chest and six-pack.

"Your lips are so soft," he moaned softly.

I kept going until I reached his dick, and teased the tip by licking and sucking on it. I deep throated him, letting my saliva release freely. I bobbed up and down slowly, and then sped up as I massaged his balls. He grabbed my head and softly guided me up and down his shaft.

"Damn ma. Fuck. Uhhh. Ahhh," he moaned.

I slid off his dick and hummed on his balls in my mouth, making him moan loud as fuck like a bitch. I stopped and went back to sucking him up as sloppily as possible, until he busted all in my mouth. I swallowed it all, and he sat up and grabbed me up. He flipped me back on my back and rushed into me.

"Tight and wet, just like I like it," he moaned in my ear.

I was wet as hell, and the sensation caused us both to shiver. We hadn't had sex since before I had Kaleeini, due to my healing time. He stroked me good as fuck, and I bit his shoulder as he kissed my neck, making me cum hard. He grabbed my hands and pinned them over my head. He slowed down his strokes and bit my bottom lip. I pushed him onto his back, and started to ride his dick.

"Ahhh Morgan baby."

I started slow, as he grabbed onto my breasts and squeezed. I placed my hand on his six-pack and started riding him like I was on the clock. I felt his dick in my throat damn near.

"Ahhhh," I moaned.

I came all over his dick, and he flipped me on all fours. I forgot I needed a red bull before fucking him. He slid into me slow, making us both moan loud as hell. I laid my head on the pillow, making sure my ass was up.

"You already know," he said in a low tone, biting his sexy lip.

He rammed into me, and all you heard was skin smacking. He lowered down and bit my shoulder as we both came together.

"Ahhhh!" we both moaned in unison.

"Damn! I love fucking you!" he said, out of breath as he kissed my back.

"You better. Forever," I smiled.

"Let's go to the pool," he smiled.

"Wha-" but before I could finish, he scooped my naked ass up and carried me to the pool. "Dreeis!" I screeched while laughing at him carrying me out.

He wore my ass out two more times, before I heard Kaleeini crying over the baby monitor. Thank God I grabbed it on the way out.

Chapter Nine: Christy Franks

Three Hours Earlier

"This shit is about to be so live," Jessica laughed as she sped down the street.

"I know bitch," I smiled.

We were headed to this party tonight that we had been planning to go to all damn year. We went every year, and this one was no different. It was just a popular ass party that everyone in the area went to every December; young Baltimore tradition. Kayden made me promise to stay in the house unless I had his cousins or Dice with me, but I was going out tonight. Thank God he was out of town on tour, so what he didn't know wouldn't hurt him. Plus, what? Am I supposed to stay in the house until they catch up with this French nigga? Nah. Nic and Morgan declined to go because I guess they do what they're told. Whatever. Kendon almost had to beat Jessica's ass, but she left anyway.

We finally pulled up to the venue that it was held at every year. The line was around the damn corner; this shit was about to be live as hell.

"Damn chica, I'm not standing in line," Jessica frowned.

"Me either, hold up," I said, strutting up to the bouncer.

"Name?" he said, looking down at me.

"Mrs. Kayden King," I said, trying my luck. I was gon' be embarrassed as fuck if he turned my ass away.

"Welcome Christy, sorry, I didn't recognize you at first," he smiled, and let Jessica and I through.

Thank God. The party was jumping already. "Pleazer" by Tyga was bumping through the speakers. This was the only party where you'd see under-aged drinking, because they really didn't give a fuck. Jessica and I started to dance to the music after we got a drink. We had so many that we were super fucked up.

"You drove Jess!" I yelled, smiling.

"Fuck Chica! Que voy a hacer!" she yelled.

Whenever she was drunk, she spoke Spanish to us. I laughed, because right now anything was funny. We continued to dance to the music, and I had my eyes closed swaying my body. Kayden's song "With It" came on, making Jessica and I scream like groupies. We really started fucking it up with our drunk asses.

"Christy!" I heard someone yell.

I turned around to see some random Asian bitch I had never met in my life. "Do I know you?" I slurred.

"We got a table upstairs, and Danielle is up there and told me to invite you guys. Why don't you come?" she smiled.

"We good, mami," Jessica slurred.

"Come on, we got free food, drinks, and everything!" she beamed.

Fuck it, I thought. Jessica and I danced our way up to the VIP, and saw a bunch of girls, food, and bottles, but no Danielle. I shrugged it off, cause I was too gone.

We plopped down on the plush couches, and just bobbed our drunk heads to the music.

"I'm so happy we came out!" I yelled to Jessica over the music.

"Yo tambien chica!" Jessica smiled.

I shrugged, cause I didn't know what the fuck she said, nor did my drunk ass care. "Turn Up the Music" by Chris Brown came on, and Jessica and I started jumping up and down, holding hands. We were turnt the fuck up, and singing the words loud as hell.

"Y'all want another drink?" that same girl asked, holding two cups prepared.

We snatched them up, downed them, and continued to dance. Jessica pulled a blunt out of her purse and lit it up. She took a pull, and passed it to me as we swayed to "Como La Flor" by Selena. This is why I loved this yearly party, cause you heard everything!

"Ayyyyy como me duele!" We sang in unison with the club. I didn't know what the fuck I was saying of course, but this was my shit!

"Nic and Morgan missed the fuck out!" I said as I blew out smoke.

She shook her head yes as she reached for the blunt. We were dancing and smoking while "Where Ya At" by Future and Drake came on. I started to feel like I had no control over my limbs. I started getting dizzy, and my head was pounding. I tried to continue to dance and ignore it, but I couldn't and stumbled onto the VIP balcony. I looked over it and the crowd was slightly blurry. I looked behind me at Jessica, and she was stumbling back and forth with her eyes closed. She fell on the floor and I rushed to her, or at least I thought I rushed. She laughed as I helped her get up. We stumbled to the couch arm in arm, and that's when I spotted the bald guy French smirking at us, with that Asian chick on his lap smirking as well. Fear and the feeling of stupidity overcame me, and I started to cry-at least it seemed like I did. I felt no tears, but I knew I was producing them. Just as Jessica and I made it to the couch, in attempt to collect our thoughts and leave, I passed out.

***

I woke up and my mouth was dry as fuck. I blinked and blinked, but it was dark as hell. My eyes started to adjust, and I tried to get up off the bed that I was in, but realized I was tied to it. I started to yell and scream as I tugged my arms and legs in attempt to free myself. A single bulb light came on, and I saw Jessica across the room still passed out on a bed. We were in someone's basement, and I didn't know who. I had never been more scared in my life. A couple seconds later, French and that girl from the club appeared from the darkness.

"Untie me muthafuckas!" I yelled.

"Well, that's not the way you ask for a favor, is it?" French smiled, showing a mouth of gold.

"Jessica!" I yelled, hoping to wake her.

French walked over and slapped the shit out of me. "Shut yo ass up!"

I started to cry. I wished I had listened to Kayden, and not snuck out to the party. I missed him so much at this moment.

"Please," I said in a low tone. I tasted blood in my mouth from the slap he gave me prior.

French sat down and began to rub his hands on my thighs. He rubbed all the way up, until he was under my dress. He leaned down and kissed my thighs, starting from my knees up to my pussy. He planted a kiss on it through my underwear. He had my legs tied far apart, so I couldn't stop him.

"Mmmm, I can't wait to try that out. Smells good," he grinned, running his tongue over his nasty teeth.

I started to cry, wondering what all he was gonna do to me. I started to worry about Jessica, cause she hadn't woke up yet.

"Kimmy, I want to see you taste her," he ordered.

I started to move frantically, hoping to loosen at least one of these ties. I still felt weak from all the alcohol I had, plus whatever they slipped in my drink; plus weed. If this hoe touched me, they better kill me because I was gon' whoop her ass once I got loose. Kimmy walked over grinning, and leaned down to kiss me. I bit the shit out of her, making her scream. French walked over and backhanded me hard as fuck, making me scream. He snatched my underwear off, ripping them.

"Now. Kimmy," he panted, out of breath, with my poor underwear dangling from his hand.

"Kimmy, no no, don't please," I tried to beg her. "You don't even know me like that! You don't want to do this!"

She lowered her head, and flicked her tongue on my clit. She went to work sucking and licking. She was good as hell at what she did, but because of the circumstances and because it was her, I wasn't turned on at all. She sped up, licking and sucking on my pussy. She dipped her tongue in my hole nice and slow. She pushed my leg up, and sucked hard on my clit.

"Ahhh. Kimmy! Please! Stop!" I begged her while crying.

She kept going as French watched, smiling from ear to ear. "Your pussy is so pretty," he said to me, folding his arms and watching Kimmy.

My body jerked as I came all over Kimmy's mouth. I was pissed as fuck! She licked me clean and dove back in, making me scream out of anger. French walked over and slapped me again. Kimmy sped up with her licks and sucks, and pushed my left leg back further. I was sensitive because of my previous orgasm, so I came again and hard. Kimmy let my leg down and came up with a smile.

"I'm gon' have some fun with y'all." French grinned as he watched Kimmy get up.

I saw Jessica wake up and realized she was tied up. French ordered Kimmy to work her magic on Jessica as he watched.

Chapter Nine: Kendon King

I woke up and saw it was 2am. I couldn't believe Jessica wasn't here; that wasn't like her. I assumed she was at her grandmother's house if she wasn't here, and laid back down. After about thirty minutes, something told me that wasn't the case. No matter how mad Jess got at me, she always came home and spent the night with me, so I knew our little argument about her going out would not cause her to not come to me.

"Fuck!" I yelled, hopping out the bed.

I was panicking like a muthafucka, cause I knew that nigga had my girl. I didn't want to call my brothers, because I knew they'd be in my ass about not being able to put my foot down with Jessica. After a couple minutes, I looked for my phone frantically to call my brothers. I didn't give a fuck; right now was not the time for me to have pride.

"Hello?" Kendrick said, obviously half sleep. I ran my hand over my low cut fade, still quiet. "Kendon," he said, due to me not responding.

"French got Jessica and Christy, man," Soon as I said it, I plopped down on the couch and put my head in my free hand.

I forgot she was even with Christy, which made me feel even worse that I hid Jessica going out from my brothers. Kayden is gon' be on a fucking murder spree if something happens to Christy. On top of that shit, we assured him that we'd make sure she was good while he was on tour.

"Nigga, what the fuck you mean he got them?! You better be fucking joking right now, Kendon!" he yelled.

Although only a year older than me, Kendrick was like a second father, and I knew he was gon' get in my ass about this shit. I wish I didn't have to call him, but I needed to save Jessica and I knew he'd be able to.

"I know man I-"

"No you don't know! That's your fucking problem, Kendon! You need to take this shit serious! Get dressed!" he yelled, and disconnected the line in my face.

Not even fifteen minutes later, Kendrick and Dreeis were at the front door banging. Soon as I opened the door, Kendrick walked in past me, headed to my living room area, and Dreeis followed. Dreeis made sure to mean mug me as he did so.

"Call Kayden please," Kendrick said to no one in particular.

Dreeis pulled out his phone and started dialing. He stepped out to tell him the news, while Kendrick and I talked.

"Where did she say she was going?" he asked while glaring at me.

"Some party. That shit they have every year around this time, at The Cave," I responded with my head down, avoiding eye contact.

"Man, what the fuck?! Why you let her go to some shit like that, at a time like this?!" he yelled.

"I told her ass she couldn't go and she went!" I yelled back.

"So what, she run y'all fucking relationship, nigga? What you say should be what goes! It shouldn't be no damn discussions, debates, or votes muthafucka! Swear to God, I feel like punching yo bitch ass!" he yelled.

"Kayden is furious man. He on a private plane right now, headed back from Detroit," Kendreeis entered the room to tell us.

"That party is over by this time, pull up Find My iPhone and see if we can locate her," Kendrick ordered.

I did as he asked, and after we waited for it to find her phone, it informed us that her phone couldn't be located, meaning it was dead or off. I called it to confirm, and it went straight to voicemail. We tried Christy after Kayden gave us her iCloud info, and the same thing.

"Fuck! Let's just go hit the pavement!" Kendrick shot up off the couch to leave, and we followed.

I couldn't believe I had let my girl get kidnapped. I felt like the weakest nigga ever. I was embarrassed, and too ashamed to even look at my brothers' faces. I prayed that my baby wasn't harmed over me acting like a damn bitch ass nigga. I deserved everything Kendrick said to me. No damn reason I should be out right now looking for my woman, cause I couldn't protect her. I was not ready to hear my father and uncle get in my ass, either. Fuck my life. I glanced at my brother from the backseat, and saw his jaw clenched hard; Kendrick was furious.

Chapter Ten: Kendrick King

I couldn't believe Kendon let Jessica go to that damn party, when we knew for a fact that this nigga wanted to kidnap our girls. He had to be out of his fucking mind to let her go. He was always letting Jessica run shit, and this time it turned out to be for the worst. I'm not saying to be her damn daddy, but learn when to put your damn foot down, especially when it's for her protection or well-being. *Got damn!* My father was gon' get in his ass. I wasn't gon' tell him, but my dad and uncle always found shit out, don't ask me how.

I flew to my condo that I kept Tia in, with my brothers in the car. Before I parked good, I hopped out. I ran up the stairs, burst in, and saw Tia hanging from the ceiling.

"Fuck!!!" I yelled.

I was trying to protect her, and this nigga found her. *Shit!* Now I had no way of finding out where the fuck French may be with Jessica and Christy. I was flying to the one spot I knew French was at, the place I mailed his people's heads to. We ran up in there, and it was cleaned out like I knew it'd be. I was panicking like a muthafucka.

"Paris!" I said, speeding to KB's. "That's pretty much her little hoe BFF. I know she would possibly know where Danielle is with French right in this moment," I said, speeding. I just hoped she and Danielle were still in contact with each other. My brothers nodded.

We arrived at KB's, and I saw Paris sitting on a customers lap.

"Excuse me," I said as I snatched her up. My brothers followed as we entered my office.

"Damn daddy. You jealous," she smiled. I had to remember that I needed her, so I wouldn't knock the shit out of her.

"Paris. Where are Danielle and French?" Kendon asked calmly.

He appeared to have tears welling up. I hated to yell and go off on him, but he needed to grow the fuck up and be a man, especially if he was gon' have a girl by his side that he needed to protect.

"I'm not sur-" I pulled my gun from my waist and placed it between her eyebrows

"You better get sure real fucking fast bitch," This nigga French had too many people protecting him. Every time someone gave us his location in the past, he had dipped by the time we arrived.

"Kendrick…Wa…wait," she stuttered. "She told me two nights ago that she was staying at Rade hotel with French."

"Any other info? If you left anything out, I'm killing you soon as I see you." I threatened.

She started to cry. "She said they were planning to kidnap your girl. I told her that if Nic ever came by or if I saw her, I would let them know. Every time I texted her that I saw Nic, she never replied, so I guess Christy and Jessica were the first they saw themselves. He planned to kidnap them all anyways! I was just in on him getting

Nic, too!" she tried to plead her case. "They're at his new house," she said, running off his address.

“Hotel or house, bitch?” I said through clenched teeth.

“House!” she replied with her eyes bucked.

It took everything inside of me not to empty this whole gun in her head. Just as she said that, I got a text from Damien letting me know he had Danielle, and giving me French’s address that she gave him. I ain’t gon’ lie, I was happy Danielle had been taken from that nigga, but I had some questions for Damien as to how he got her.

"Get the fuck up and direct us to his house, and it better be right!" Kendon yelled.

***

We arrived at his house, and all the lights were off.

"He better be here, Paris," I told her, just to scare her dumb ass. I already knew he was here, because Damien confirmed the address she had given us prior.

"She said they live here together, so they should be here," she replied with a shaken voice.

We all hopped out and walked slowly up his driveway. Dumb ass nigga had no security, guards, homies, nothing. This nigga was living it up, so he didn't feel the need to watch his bitch ass back.

"Knock on the fucking door, and make like you visiting!" Kendreeis ordered.

We stood to the side as Paris knocked on the door. After about five minutes and about three more knocks, we heard footsteps. I looked at my brothers, letting them know to make sure their guns were ready. Some random chick opened the door, and we rushed her quietly. I grabbed her and covered her mouth. I held my gun to her head as my brothers looked around the dark living room.

"Where is ya boy French? I'm gon' take my hand off your mouth; if you scream, I'm killing your ass right now."

"Downstairs in the basement," she whispered once I removed my hand.

We walked downstairs, and I heard him in the basement yelling at some girls who I'm sure were Christy and Jessica.

"Thanks," was all I said before I pumped one in old girl's dome.

I let her fall out my arms slow, cause I didn't want her to make a thump sound. I pushed Paris towards the door to make sure she didn't run off. We burst in, and I saw some hoe down between Jessica's legs eating her pussy. What the fuck was going on in this muthafucka? French tried to run for his gun, and I shot him in the stomach. I didn't want to kill him just yet. He fell to the ground, and I shot his kneecaps as Kendon and Kendreeis untied Christy and Jessica. The bitch that was licking on Jessica ran her dumb ass to French's side, holding his head up.

"Get the fuck up!" I ordered calmly, but irritated. What hoe in their right mind gon' side with the nigga with no weapon? He really had these bitches gone.

"French! Baby!" she yelled, ignoring me.

"Get your dumb ass up 'for I lay your ass out right here!" I yelled, making her jump.

Kendon helped Jessica and Christy to the car. Kendreeis put a bullet in the dumb hoe's head, then helped Kendon with the women. I looked over at Paris and shot her in the head. Stupid bitch, trying to get Nic kidnapped and thought she was gon' live? Nah. The pussy was good, but not that good.

I looked over to my right, and saw some brake fluid cans. I started emptying them, one by one, all over the floor. I saw French try to stand up, catching on to what I was gonna do. I shot his ass in the shoulder. I wanted to make sure he was immobile, but not dead so he could burn alive. After emptying all four cans everywhere, I took a match out my pocket, lit it, and threw it on the ground by him and Paris. He started squirming and trying to move away. I stood in the doorway to make sure the floor was burning correctly. I closed the door and smiled once I heard French's screams. I turned the eyes of the stove all the way up, and threw another lit match on the brake fluid, soaked carpet. I ran outside to the car with Kendreeis, Kendon, Jessica, and Christy. I sat there for a bit, and after about thirty seconds, the house went up in flames and I pulled off. I killed this nigga with no words exchanged between he an I; it was perfect.

***

It was about 4am when I got home, and a sense of relief came over me. I smiled thinking about how Kendon tore into Jessica after making sure she was okay; about time. We dropped Christy off at the airport our private jets take off from, to give her to Kayden. He decided to bring her along while he finished off his tour. I don't blame him; every nigga felt no one could protect his woman like he could.

I walked up the stairs slowly, and walked into KJ's room. He was sleep on his stomach with his cover on. I hoped our new baby was as calm and well behaved as he was. I laughed at my thought. I headed to the room I shared with my love, and began to pull off my clothes.

"Is everything okay now?" Nic asked as soon as I sat on the edge of the bed.

"Yeah. We got that nigga finally. And tell your mom Danielle is safe," I said, taking my small gold chain off.

"Oh, okay good. Thank God!"

"Which means we can get married Sunday," I said, cuddling up behind her excitedly.

She turned around to face me. "Really?" she asked, caressing my face.

"Yeah, I promised you after we got him, right?"

She shook her head yes, and smiled big as hell. It made me feel good to make her smile like that. I placed my hand over her stomach to feel our new baby coming, and she put hers on top of mine. She kissed my lips and turned her back to me so I could hug her from behind.

***

Nic and I were finally married, and after our honeymoon in Paris, we decided to go on a group trip to Vegas with Kendreeis, Kendon, Kayden, Damien, Morgan, Jessica, Christy, and Danielle. My father and uncle decided to come out of retirement temporarily, while my brothers and I had a good time. I told him I could stay, but he said a happy wife makes a happy life, and if going to Vegas and Paris made Nic happy, I needed to do it. I agreed with him, too.

We landed our private jet around 6pm in Las Vegas, NV, and the city was gorgeous. The warmth of the weather felt good as hell as Nic and I walked off the runway hand in hand. I watched her long hair blow in the slight wind, and the way she smiled and laughed made me feel good. After all that we had been through, it was Heaven on earth to see her smile and be happy. At this moment, it seemed as if nothing else mattered in the world but her beautiful face and warm laughter. She saw me staring at her as we approached the doorway of the port, and she kissed my lips.

"I love you, Mr. King," she said, wiping her lipstick off my lips.

"I love you too, baby girl," I told her, half smiling.

"I'm so ready to turn the fuck up!" Jessica yelled, making us laugh.

"Not too much, my wife is pregnant," I smiled as we walked through the port to the limo.

"She's only about 3 months, she can drink still." Morgan joked, and we laughed as we go into the limo.

We arrived at Caesar's Palace and helped the bellhop with our bags. We checked into the hotel, and headed up to our rooms. The suites we got were out of this world.

"I love this!" Nic beamed as she belly hopped onto the bed back first. "Mmmmm! These sheets feel so good."

"Do they?"

"Yes. Not better than the sheets in Paris, though."

"I see you've upgraded your tastes since I met you," I smiled.

"Well, I can't have a flashy man and still be shopping at Forever 21," she cheesed.

"Yeah, I am pretty fly. But you make cheap shit look expensive," I said, pulling her off the bed into my arms. We kissed each other's lips for a bit, and basked in the moment of silence. I was so lucky to have Nic, and I knew she felt the same.

"I'm going to call your mother real quick and check on Kendrick," she said, grabbing her iPhone.

After she did, we looked around the room some more and looked out the window over the pretty city. "Where we going tonight? Y'all not even old enough to get in anywhere," I laughed.

"Actually I have a fake ID, but we were just going to go to dinner tonight, and maybe walk the strip," she said, wrapping her arms around my neck.

We arrived at Le Cirque, and everybody was dressed up. I had on a three-piece Armani suit in burgundy, with an all-black Armani button-up. Nic looked beautiful as usual in a black, strapless dress that was long in the back and short in the front. It was lined in burgundy like my suit, and she had in burgundy sandal stilettos to match. Her long hair was curled, and hanging down her back. We sat down at the table and I looked around, feeling thankful for everybody that was here, even Danielle's wild ass. Morgan and Kendreeis were constantly exchanging pecks, like some hot young teenagers.

"Did y'all not have enough time together in the room?" Christy asked.

"I'm saying," Kendon chimed in, and we all laughed.

I could get used to this. Being with my peoples, enjoying the good life. Making my lady happy, and actually enjoying all the damn money I make. I was wealthy as hell– not rich, but wealthy–and I needed to enjoy it. I was going to enjoy it. It had been too long since we all had time to chill out together. Every time I looked up, I was fighting somebody off, whether it was Trenton, Houston, or nasty ass French.

"You okay?" Nic asked, snapping me out of my thoughts, and kissing my neck.

"Don't start that," I told her, referring to the neck kiss. She just smiled and kissed my lips.

We enjoyed the dinner, and walked the strip since the ladies couldn't go into the clubs. They swore that tomorrow we were gon' try, since they had their fake IDs, but I doubted it. They said we could tell the bouncers Nic was Naya Rivera, Morgan was Cassie, and Christy was Lauren London. Afterwards, we retired to our suites, and I wore Nic's ass out. Tonight was the first night that I had actually slept peacefully, and I could get used to it.

Chapter Ten: Kendreeis King

After chilling with my brothers and friends at Jules house, I decided to head home. It felt good to just chill and not have to devise a plan to capture a fuckin enemy for once. It was almost like a continuation of our Vegas trip. It wasn't too late, but I wanted to get home at a reasonable time to my girl. I meant what I said to Morgan when I told her that I was going to make sure I balanced this street shit and my personal life with her. I didn't want to be one of those dudes that left their girl at home alone 22 hours of the day. That's how she ended up riding another dick.

I smiled at the thought of her. Before Morgan, I was angry and bitter. I wasn't quite sure why, but that was my personality. I didn't give a fuck about shit but my bread, and how to make more of it. Morgan was a blessing in disguise, and I was more than thankful for her and my son.

I stopped at a red light and decided to send her a text.

Me: You up beautiful?

Wifey: Of course, you know I can't go to sleep without you daddy.

I smiled at her response, and put my phone away. As I waited for the light to turn green, an all-black escalade pulled up on the side of me. Before I could look over good, the front passenger let off a round of bullets into my car.

Chapter Eleven: July Woods

I didn't say much this whole time, but I was furious when them holier than thou niggas killed my baby daddy Trenton. Then, when I finally found happiness again in Harley, they offed him too. They thought life was sweet I bet; that's funny. Since my life was hell, I planned to make theirs and their bitches lives hell as well. I was 25 with no job since I couldn't strip anymore, and a new baby with a dead baby daddy. I had no friends either, since Paris and Gina disappeared. Oh yeah, I was gon' ruin them bitches one by one.

I especially hated Christy's crazy ass. She is the reason my nigga is gone. She is the reason for a lot of things. Trenton and me were doing great until she decided to leave him. I thought it was a good thing, until that nigga started tripping. That's all he talked about, and that's all he wanted; bum ass Christy. To top it all off, she put hands on me in the club in front of everyone.

I called my sisters and twin brother, who lived an Atlanta, to come help me end them muthafuckas, and they agreed. April and Adrienne were twins sisters, and ruthless as hell, not to mention beautiful. Soon as them King brothers laid eyes on them, they'd be putty in their hands. Who'd be able to deny twins that looked like Christina Milian? Let me know when you figure that out.

Anyway, I had so much shit that would fuck their lives up, that it made me smile at random times. As for my twin brother June, once he heard me crying on the phone about being a single mother cause of these niggas, he was on the first thing smoking. I was so excited to have my sisters come out here and join my brother and I. By the time we finish, we will be infamous for taking that whole clan down. Get ready muthafuckas. By the way, it wasn't French who hung Tia's snake ass! Ahhahahahahhahahahahahhahahah.

Last release:

Finding A Loyal Love

Check out our upcoming releases on the next page!

To submit a manuscript for our review, email us at leosullivanpresents@gmail.com

Join our mailing list to get a notification for these upcoming releases!

CPSIA information can be obtained at www.ICGtesting.com
Printed in the USA
LVOW07s2048151015

458418LV00026B/1027/P